Lifestyles
of the
RICH
and
SHAMELESS

W9-BYF-965

Also By Kiki Swinson

Wifey

I'm Still Wifey

Life After Wifey

The Candy Shop

A Sticky Situation

Still Wifey Material

Playing Dirty

Notorious

Sleeping with the Enemy (with Wahida Clark)

Heist (with De'nesha Diamond)

Also by Noire

Maneater (with Mary B. Morrison)

Published by Kensington Publishing Corp.

Lifestyles
of the
RICH
and
SHAMELESS

KIKI SWINSON
NOIRE

Kensington Publishing Corp.
http://www.kensingtonbooks.com

First trade paperback printing: December 2011

ISBN-13: 978-0-7582-5180-0
ISBN-10: 0-7582-5180-7

10 9 8 7 6 5 4 3 2 1

Printed in the United States of America

Contents

Shamelessly Rich

Kiki Swinson

Prologue

My Worst Mistake

Blood. There was so much blood everywhere. It was clouding my vision. And the smell. It was so strong and overwhelming. The smell was one I could never forget.

"Aggghhh!" I screamed as my body moved involuntarily. I didn't even realize I was jumping up and down. The sight in front of me was ghastly and I thought I would go into shock. I had stood by and done nothing and now I was going to pay for it. *We* were going to pay dearly for it, I should say.

"Megan, shut the fuck up! If you scream again it's over! I put a bullet in his ass and end this whole shit," Eric yelled at me. His face was contorted into a scowl I had never seen him wear before. One of his fists was clenched tightly and his other hand gripped a gun so hard that his knuckles were pale. I knew he meant business, so I tried to obey his demands. I clasped my hands over my mouth, trying to keep the screams in. It didn't work. As I looked down again, trying to muffle a scream proved futile. I was brimming with emotion. This whole shit was out of control now.

"What did you do?" I belted out through wracking sobs. I could feel my face swelling from all of the crying I had been doing. There was blood everywhere—on the floor, on the table, some had even squirted on the wall. It was clear that our victim needed medical attention, and fast. I stared at the almost lifeless form in front of me. Things had gone terribly wrong. Eric had gone berserk punching and kicking and hitting. It was supposed to be easy. There wasn't supposed to be any violence involved, just a snatch, grab, and collect. "Oh God, Eric . . . What did you do?" I hollered again.

"I did what we planned to do! Remember whose fuckin' idea this was in the first place. Now shut the fuck up and get on the phone and make them believe us now!" Eric growled cruelly. I knew he was right. This had all been my idea. All for revenge. I never meant for it to turn out like this.

"Start fuckin' movin'! I'm gonna snap the fuckin' pictures of his half-dead ass. Just in case they don't believe that this shit is serious," Eric continued in the same cruel, ruthless voice as before. It amazed me how he could just stand in a pool of a helpless person's blood and not even care. Eric was definitely not the man I thought he was. My vision had been clouded. Too clouded.

"I—I . . . can't!" I wailed. My stomach was cramping and my entire body trembled. I couldn't stop staring at the victim. I couldn't help but think that this was all my fault. I had done all of this to myself and to my family. Now here I stood feeling like the worst person alive. Now I wanted to just save him— take him and run far away from Eric and his goons that were outside. I wanted to ask for forgiveness for being such a selfish and spoiled little bitch.

4

"Help me . . . Me . . . gan," he whispered weakly through his bloody, battered lips. That broke my heart. I was so happy he was still alive, but his words and hearing him rasp out my name sent a pang of hurt throughout my body and a cold chill down my spine. How could I have done something so wretched to my own flesh and blood?

"Shut the fuck up! She can't help you. The only one that can help you is your accountant!" Eric barked, rushing over to where I stood. I shot Eric an evil look. I wanted to kill him with my bare hands. All this time, I'd thought I was in love with Eric, but I realized right then that I was just infatuated with his bad boy style and the things he represented.

Being with Eric had been like a walk on the wild side for me . . . like an adventure. Being born with a silver spoon in my mouth wasn't enough. I had grown bored with growing up wealthy and having everything at my disposal. From the time I could remember, I'd had everything. And I do mean *everything*. I guess all of the international trips, the private school education, high-priced gifts for doing absolutely nothing at all, having enough money at my disposal that I could afford to lose thousands at a time and not even care and having every material thing that I wanted just wasn't enough for me. I was still bored as hell. By the time I was eighteen, I wanted more.

I went out with a ghetto bad boy for the thrill of it. Eric was the complete opposite of me. He had grown up dirt poor and his story was stereotypical of what my parents had tried to keep me away from—Eric's mother was on crack, his father was never in the picture, and he was raised by a grandmother who was in such bad health that she couldn't discipline him or keep up with him. He was a street hustler by the time he was fifteen years old and he came from the worst part of Virginia Beach. Although Eric was just thirty-one, he had already done two stints in prison. I had thought of him as such an adventure. Not to mention that all of the hot sex, ecstasy pills, and weed, run-ins with the law and making other girls jealous also excited me about Eric. Every chick in Virginia Beach wanted a piece of Eric Chambers, but he had chosen me. That made me feel more special than any gift my father could have ever given me. But look where my stupid infatuation and need for a walk on the wild side led to.

"You think I'm fuckin' playing, right?" Eric hissed, walking over and kicking the already defenseless victim in the side.

"Aggh!" he screamed out in pain. I had not even realized I was daydreaming and hesitating to make the call. "Stop it! You said you wouldn't hurt him!" I screeched. The tears were uncontrollable now.

"Bitch, if you don't pick up the phone and dial somebody to get the money, I will fuckin' kill him and pin all this shit on you! Or better yet, I might just kill your ass too," Eric barked. His face was so serious. I knew when he was bluffing and this wasn't one of those moments. I knew that if I didn't do it, Eric would be committing murder for real.

My hands were trembling fiercely as I dialed the familiar number. I clutched my cell phone tightly against my ear and prayed that the accountant answered. Eric was standing over me menacingly as he brandished his gun so both of us could see it.

"Hello," I breathed into the phone through the computerized voice disguiser. I swallowed hard when I recognized the familiar voice on the message service that picked up. I felt like

I would piss on myself. Eric snatched the phone from me. He could see that I had frozen up like a deer caught in headlights.

"We want three million in cash for his release. We ain't callin' again! If you involve the cops, he dies. No second chances!" Eric screamed into the phone.

My heart sank as I looked into the battered face of my own father. I felt a sickening mixture of emotions. Part anger, part regret, and a large part fear. I wished we weren't at this point. I wished my parents had hidden their disapproval of my wild life instead of treating me so badly. In time, we could've worked it out. But we didn't, so I set up this scheme to get revenge. I'd wanted them to hurt as much as I did, but now I see that I was being greedy and self-centered. Damn, I wished that I could rewind time.

1

My Twenty-first Birthday

"Thank you, Daddy!" I squealed as I raced over to my brand new apple red sparkly Range Rover. The new vehicle gleamed so brightly I had to put on my Gucci shades to look at it in the bright sun. I rushed around it, peeking into the windows and examining every inch of my new toy. "Oh my God! Daddy! You had it all custom kitted just for me!" I said excitedly as I peered into the window and looked at the interior. My father had had my new Range tricked out in a shiny, metallic red, custom exterior paint that had sparkles in it. He'd also put the Range on twenty-two-inch chrome rims with the same red paint splashed between the rim spokes. The inside was tan leather with red piping around the seats and my initials embroidered in red on the headrests. It was definitely something nobody else in Virginia Beach would have. My father knew how to please his baby girl.

"You are the *best* daddy a girl could have!" I squealed, throwing my arms around his neck and squeezing him.

My father was smiling and shaking his head proudly. He

broke up our embrace and looked at me lovingly. "Happy Birthday, baby girl," he said as he extended his hand with the keys. He knew looking at it from the outside was killing me.

I snatched the keys from him and hurriedly unlocked the door of my new whip. Once inside, the new car smell filled my nostrils and I felt like I was in heaven. It had everything imaginable and I was already picturing the jealous stares I would get. This car was definitely going to make a statement around town. Smiling from ear to ear, I said, "I'm ready to go! Can I go show off?"

"You need to drive responsibly," my father said seriously as he leaned into my driver side window. "Now that you're twenty-one and old enough to drink . . . I want you to think like an adult. No drinking and driving, no speeding, no—"

"Daddy," I whined, cutting him off. "Don't spoil my happy moment with one of your lectures," I said. I was still cheesing from ear to ear.

"Megan, your mother and I worry about you. I just want you to be responsible . . . please," he said, not letting up. I heard him, but I wasn't trying to hear him. He was right about one thing. I was twenty-one now and old enough to drink and do as I pleased.

"What time are you coming home, young lady?" my mother chimed in, sticking her smiling face into the passenger side window of my ride. I hadn't even noticed her walk up to us. Looking at my mother was like looking into a mirror. I was every bit the spitting image of her. We were both your typical biracial-looking types with long dark hair and light brown eyes. I stood about two inches taller than her at five feet and six inches, but that didn't take anything away from my mother's model looks. Plus, with the help of my mother's plastic surgeon, she and I both had the most perfect C cup breasts and Brazilian butt lifts you'd ever seen on a mother/daughter pair. My mother had definitely let me indulge in some of her vices, like plastic surgery and wearing revealing clothes. My father didn't always agree, but he didn't wield much power in my house. People often mistook my mother and me for Kim Kardashian and her mother when we were out. We always found it so amusing. I mean, we did have just as much, or more money than the Kardashians, so they weren't too far off. Personally, I thought I looked a little prettier than Kim, and my mother, well, she had not one single wrinkle popping up like Kim Kardashian's mother, who in my opinion needed more Botox.

"Megan, you haven't answered my question," my mother reminded me. I had avoided it on purpose. She was such a worry wart. I knew how to get her to back off though.

"Well, you know I have to show off and take this baby for a spin around Virginia Beach. I have to show Krista and her mom. You know they'll just die when they see it," I said, wickedly gauging my mother's reaction. Her face softened and I could tell she had bought my story. "I promise to be home at a decent hour," I assured her. I knew that any mention of making someone in Virginia Beach jealous would back her down. She was in a competition with Mrs. Boyd, my used-to-be best friend Krista's mom. My mother would agree to anything to get Mrs. Boyd jealous or to show her up.

"Make sure you blow your horn in that bitch's driveway," my mother said evilly.

"I'm headed there right now," I replied. I was lying like no tomorrow. I had no plans on seeing Krista or showing her mother my new whip. Krista and I had stopped speaking months ago. We no longer had shit in common. I planned to be out all night to make sure everybody, especially my haters, got to see my whip. My mother gave me another stern warning and my father gave me a kiss on my cheek. They both stepped away from the truck as I peeled out of our circular driveway. I was on my way to see my new man and to make a few hood-rat bitches very upset.

I looked down at my T-shirt, which read *Shamelessly Rich,* and smirked to myself. That was an understatement. I was unbelievably spoiled and damn sure wasn't ashamed to be rich. My last name was Rich and it was more than just a coincidence. I was definitely born into a *rich* family. I was the only child of one of the wealthiest men in Virginia. By the time I was born, my father, Gavin Rich, was a well-known business tycoon who had clawed his way to the top of the Forbes list. Not only did he own a string of Shell gas stations in more than ten states, he had cornered the market on Virginia Beach beachfront properties and high-rises before the housing market crashed. My father was one of the shrewdest businessmen around. Some people said he was even more cutthroat than Donald Trump.

My father, a German immigrant who initially came to America on a student visa but elected to stay after he finished all of his studies, met my mother, the beautiful Priscilla Rich, while they both attended Columbia University. My father disowned his family when they had a problem with my mother being half black and half Italian. Both of my parents were well educated. They dated while they pursued master's degrees in business management and accounting. All of this was before

I was born, of course. By the time I came along, my father had already made a boatload of money. A friend of his had told him about an opportunity to buy a gas station in Virginia Beach and the rest is history. I have heard the story so many times about how my father jumped at the opportunity. He and my mother took out a business loan and borrowed money from her family so they could make the venture happen. Once everything was finalized, they moved to the suburbs of Virginia Beach. Let's just say he made many more great business decisions after that and I was the benefactor of them all.

I never knew a day where I wanted for anything. If I even looked at something hard it was mine right after. My father spent a fortune to make me happy. He always said I would be taking over the lead on his businesses, but I was not interested in that shit at all. I was satisfied taking what I needed from him. Everyone around town knew who I was. From the time I was in grade school, I was nicknamed the "rich" girl. The irony is still lost on some people. Most women envied me while the men wanted to be seen with me. I had my pick of the litter. I probably could have stolen a grown-ass man from his wife.

Twenty minutes later, I eased the Range Rover down the crowded street of one of the worst neighborhoods in Virginia Beach. I knew all eyes would be on me. I blew my horn loudly and the crowd of street hustlers that were all posted up against an abandoned house all turned around and glared in the direction of my Range. I could see them ducking their heads and squinting their eyes to see who was coming through their hood in such a fly-ass whip. I blew the horn again as I pulled up slowly to the decrepit house. Some of the hustlers put their hands on their waistbands in a show of defense; that's when I knew I had to hurry up and identify myself before my ass ended up filled with holes.

"What's up, Eric? Hey, boo!" I sang out as I bent my head and peeked out the window. All of the dudes out there were staring at me now.

Eric had his mouth hung open in shock. He couldn't believe his eyes. It didn't take him long to change that shocked looked into a huge smile. "Dayum, rich girl! Ya daddy was trickin' on that ass again," Eric said, showing all his pearly whites as he bopped over to me. He put his face in the window and planted the most sloppy tongue kiss on me. I knew it was all a show for his little street thug friends.

"Mmmm, I like the way that tastes," I said as we pulled away from each other. I inhaled his scent and it was intoxicating. The mixture of cologne and his bad boy swag had me ready to jump his damn bones right then and there.

Eric smiled and raced around to the passenger side of the Range. "See y'all niggahs later," he yelled out. I laughed as I looked at the jealous, hungry-looking faces of his street counterparts.

"Where we going, Daddy?" I asked seductively. I knew damn well where we were going. It wasn't a secret what Eric and I did each time we were together now. I didn't mind at all either.

"Our regular spot," Eric said as he leaned over and looked into the backseat of the car. He was giving it the once-over like he still couldn't believe it. "This shit right here is tight. You need to be careful rolling through the hood in this shit though. It ain't safe in these parts. Niggahs will definitely carjack your little ass for a ride like this," he warned. I waved him off like he was being ridiculous.

"They know I'm your girl. They won't mess with me," I replied.

Eric started laughing. Then he mimicked my words with a proper accent, which was the total opposite of how he regularly spoke. "Yo, you sound like a straight white chick. You look like a spoiled rich girl. Come the fuck on. Please, Megan, don't be stupid. Them hungry niggahs will do your ass in and send your body home to your daddy in a minute. Basically, you need me," he said, turning his head toward the window. He had shut me down. Sometimes he could be so cruel. I hated when he was mad at me or wasn't speaking to me. I always wanted to keep him happy. I was nervous now. If Eric was mad at me things wouldn't be right. I had to fix it. We drove in silence, both of us thinking.

Eric Chambers was my new man. I had met him at a party one of the nights that I was supposed to be spending at Krista's house. Eric was a tall, dark, handsome, six foot, chocolate specimen of a man. He was ten years older than me so I knew I could never take him home to my parents. He also wasn't exactly the type of man my parents had envisioned for me either. Eric had done hard prison time and was a petty drug dealer, but I was full on in love with him. His dick was thick and it was good. At twenty-one, I was as sexually adept as a forty-year-old woman. At least I thought so. I had had sex with plenty little boys in my private school. I had even fucked a few of my father's older business associates, but there was nothing that could compare to Eric's dick and the way he ate my pussy out every single time we were together. I was clearly in love. I never wanted to be apart from him and I made sure I saw him every day. My parents thought I was in classes at college, but I didn't have time for school. In my assessment, I didn't need a college education. I was a Rich!

"Where you going?" Eric asked, breaking our silence. He had seen me pass our usual luxury hotel rendezvous spot.

"It's a surprise," I said, smiling at him. I was just glad he was speaking to me again.

"I gotta get back out there to get some paper so I don't really have time for surprises today," he said, annoyed. I knew what that meant. He was always threatening me with leaving and going back out on the street. Eric knew how to hit me where it counted.

"Look in my bag. There is enough money in there to take care of you for today," I said nervously. I didn't want to think about him breaking up our time together. He knew it too. This wasn't the first time he made me feel anxious enough to give up some cash to keep him with me.

"Nah . . . I ain't taking your money," he said.

I knew he was lying. I sucked my teeth. I stopped the car and grabbed my Hermès Birkin bag. I dug inside and pulled out a wad of cash.

"I think this is about eight hundred dollars . . . my daytime spending money. You can have it. I will go get more after we leave our spot," I said, forcefully pushing the cash in Eric's direction. He looked at me and, feigning reluctance, he took the money . . . just like I knew he would. I mean, how could he refuse, pussy and money?

"Make sure you hit me off with more later. This ain't enough. I'm sayin' I make this in an hour outside beatin' that block," Eric said. I believed him too. There were so many fiends running around the part of Virginia Beach that he lived in it was not even funny.

I finally pulled the Range up to Reed's, a well-known, high-end jewelry store in Virginia. Eric looked at me strangely.

"This was my surprise. I got a gift today and I want to give you one," I said. I bent over and kissed his thick lips. "It's my birthday, but I want to make you happy too. C'mon," I demanded playfully. I rushed out of the car.

Eric got out of the car in silence. I grabbed his arm and we walked into Reed's arm in arm like a married couple. That shit made me feel so grown up. When we got inside, the old white lady behind the counter gave Eric a once-over and kind of turned up her nose. I squinted my eyes at her evilly. This wrinkled bitch didn't know who she was fucking with. I hated when people automatically stereotyped people and thought they didn't have money. I knew what to do to fix that bitch. I walked over to the watch case.

"Excuse me, ma'am. I want that thirty-five millimeter, mother-of-pearl face, Oyster Perpetual Rolex, please," I sang. The woman's face dropped. She was so surprised that I knew the name and style of such an expensive watch without even flinching. Little did she know my father had at least five different Rolexes. The woman slowly moved toward the watch counter, still seemingly taken aback, but she knew her commission depended on me.

"Honey, extend your wrist so she can fit it on," I said snidely, holding eye contact with the woman. Eric raised one eyebrow but he didn't hesitate to stretch his arm out. The old woman's hands were shaking as she fiddled with the watch and

Eric's arm. She widened her eyes when she saw all of his tattoos. I was laughing inside. This lady was probably in brain overload trying to figure us out. Once Eric had the watch on I grabbed his arm to examine it. I sized it up, moving it into the light so I could see better or more like so I could rub the shit in her old wrinkled face.

"Do you like this one?" I asked Eric.

"You damn right. This shit right here is tight business," he said, putting his arm in several different angles so he could see how it looked.

"We'll take it," I said, slamming my American Express plum card down on the counter. The old woman looked like she would faint. "Oh, did you need identification?" I asked, before the old bitch could even try to make a case that we were there to commit credit card fraud. She couldn't even get her words out before I flicked my driver's license at her. The old woman rushed around the counter trying to ring up my purchase. I walked over to the diamond showcase and picked out a bracelet for myself. I didn't need it, nor did I really want it, but I had a point to prove. After the lady rang everything up and handed me my $14,000 receipt, I scribbled my name and smirked at her.

"You should never judge a book by its cover . . . bitch!" I snapped as I snatched my bag and turned my back on her.

"You a wild girl, Megan. That ol' bitch ain't know what to do," Eric laughed. I was glad he was smiling.

"Now off to the Westin . . . I need some of that good good," I said to him sweetly. All was good now.

* * *

I could barely keep my hands off Eric as we kissed and fumbled with each other's clothes until we almost fell into the hotel room. I was hot and wanted him so badly. He backed me up until I was on the luxurious, king-sized, heavenly bed that only Westin was known for. Eric had his tongue almost down my throat. I was moaning, hot and heavy. He practically ripped my shirt off me and exposed my perfect tits.

"Wait . . . you need these," he said, stopping to pull a little packet of ex out of his pocket. Eric knew just what I needed to take me over the top. I laughed and grabbed the pills from him. I raced over to the little wet bar and cracked open one of the four-dollar bottles of water they beat you in the head for. I took three ecstasy pills this time, when I usually only took two.

"Whoa, whoa . . . Don't be OD-ing on those shits," Eric warned.

I sexily began removing my jeans as if I was doing a striptease for him. I wanted the pills to hurry up and take effect so when he touched me it would feel electrifying. Eric stepped out of his jeans and pulled his boxers off too. I smiled. I dropped to my knees and crawled over to him like a lioness. He had his ten-inch hunk of manhood in his hand and I put my face right up on it. Eric swiped his dick across my lips, teasing me. I sat back on my feet like a dog ready to beg. He laughed. I started feeling real tingly. The pills were taking hold. I liked my lips seductively and then let a glob of saliva fall from my mouth onto his dick.

"Yeah," he whispered. His words even sent chills over my body. Now the ex was in full effect. I opened my mouth wide and took every inch of his dick inside my hot lips. I gagged a little bit as Eric grabbed my head forcefully and began fucking my face.

"Mmm," I moaned. I could feel my pussy pulsating. I wanted him and I wanted him badly. I moved up and down on his dick vigorously. He was moving his hips as well.

"Urgh," he growled. I knew what that meant. I moved off him for a minute.

"Cum in my mouth," I moaned out.

"Open it now!" he grumbled, and his legs seemed to get weak. I took him back into my mouth. "Aggghh!" he belted out as he let a hot load of cum into the back of my throat. I pulled his dick out and opened my mouth so he could see that his cum was on my tongue. Then I closed my eyes and swallowed it all. I licked my lips like a real porn star.

"You get down like a grown-ass woman," Eric huffed.

I got up and got on the bed. I looked at him as I let my legs scissor open. Eric knew what that meant. He bent down and buried his face right in my pussy. I swear his mouth sent a million needle stabs of hot sparks all over me.

"Y-e-s!" I hissed. I was moving my head in circles because the ecstasy had me "rolling" now and I couldn't help it. All of my senses were heightened. Eric was devouring my clit. Then he moved his head down and inserted his tongue deep into my pussy hole. "This is why I won't ever let your ass go!" I screamed. I was panting now. I was pushing my pussy onto his tongue with vigor. "Mmmm," I moaned out. I could feel an orgasm welling up inside me. Just as I was about to cum, Eric stopped. I popped my eyes open, but before I could complain he drove his dick into me so hard my pussy made a loud farting noise. Eric began slamming into me and it hurt so damn good.

"Whose pussy is this, rich girl?" he huffed. At first I didn't answer. My tongue and my brain weren't even on the same page. But, the more I kept my answer to myself the harder Eric pounded into me. "I said whose pussy is this, rich girl?" he barked. My words got caught in my throat. He slammed even harder into my pelvis.

"It's yours, Eric! It's your pussy!" I screamed out after my brain finally sent the message to my tongue. Every nerve in my body could be felt. It felt so good. I don't know how I ever had sex in the past without the use of ecstasy. "Ahhhh!" I screamed as I busted my own nut. Eric followed right after. He collapsed next to me. When his dick fell out of my sloppy wet pussy, I got up and jumped right back on it.

"Damn . . . you're like a fuckin' fiend when you on that ex . . . a niggah can't keep up with you, rich girl," he huffed and puffed.

"That's okay . . . I can keep up with you though," I whispered as I slid up and down on his dick. He smiled and let me take control. Just how I liked it.

2

My Fair Warning

Two years had passed just like that. I was now twenty-three years old and under all types of pressure from my parents. They continued to make threats and I continued to do my thing. I would slow down for a minute, but as soon as they let their guard down I'd be back at it. Soon enough, every day was a constant power struggle with them. They were continuously hounding me about college and about learning to work the family business. The day my father found out I had been lying about attending college all of that time, he hit the fucking roof. Education was the single most important thing to his ass.

Too bad I wasn't interested in becoming the CEO of his fucking gas station and real estate empire. Why would I learn the business? I didn't plan on working a day in my life. My father had seen to it that I wouldn't have to, at least that's what he always promised. I couldn't understand why he was changing up the game on me and hounding me to go to school. Honestly, my main concern had become the boatloads of cash at my disposal and keeping Eric laced with cash and gifts. Making him happy in turn made me happy. I was used to living a life where I did as I pleased. My parents weren't going to change that shit now.

Unlike my parents, I was sure school just wasn't my thing. I had no aspirations to go back, although I told my father that I had gone back for a few classes so I could keep him off my back. He wrote a check to the school and I got it right back in a refund since I didn't register for any classes. I was also not interested in anything that remotely resembled or even seemed close to work. My job was to shop, hang out all night at nightclubs, get fucked by Eric, and trick a little dough on him so he stayed put. Period. Eric was now the regular driver of the Range and because of that very fact I got to see him much more often. We had been going strong for two years . . . a miracle for me since I never had a man past three or four months. I must admit, being with Eric was like being in a money pit. I must've spent close to a million dollars on him in the first year we were together, so imagine the totality of the damage I had done in two years.

BANG! BANG! "Megan! Open this door right now!"

I was jolted out of an alcohol-induced sleep. I heard my father yelling from outside the estate guesthouse, which is where I had been residing for the past year. With my parents being extra strict and on my back, I had moved out of the main house so I'd have more privacy and freedom to come and go as I pleased. My father was banging on the door again like whatever he wanted couldn't wait.

"Ugghh," I winced as the pounding in my head became

readily apparent as soon as I forced my leaden eyelids open. He banged on the door again. The sound sent a reverberating quake through my skull.

"Shhh," I hissed, although I knew he couldn't hear me. The feeling in my head and my stomach was what I would imagine near-death to feel like. Can you say hangover? I squinted and looked around. The room was semidark, all of the shades were pulled, which I was grateful for since the sun would've probably sent the sick feeling I was experiencing over the top. I touched my chest and legs as my father pounded again with even more force than the first time. I was still in my party clothes—a very skimpy miniskirt and an even skimpier tank. I couldn't let him see me like that, but it was clear he wasn't going away. Somehow he knew I was at home, although my car wasn't parked outside.

"Megan Rich! I'm giving you one minute!" he barked, hitting the door again.

"Fuck!" I cursed with the incessant pounding in my head growing worse. I got up as fast as I could with that horrible headache and scrambled to the master bedroom for my robe. I couldn't let him see me dressed like a damn streetwalker. I was a saint in my father's eyes and that's how I wanted to keep it. I rushed from the bedroom toward the sound of yet another barrage of door poundings. "I'm coming!" I screamed, but immediately regretted it when the pulsating in my head and the pain hit me. I pulled myself slowly through the house and barely made it to the door. I snatched it back with a mean scowl on my face. "Why are you banging on the door like you're crazy?" I growled with my eyebrows furrowed.

My father had the fist of his right hand balled up and something in his left hand. His face was contorted in a way I had probably never seen displayed before, except of course, when his stocks and investments took a dive. He looked scary as hell. I think I could safely say he was angrier than I've ever seen him before. He stormed his six-foot, two-inch, slightly over-weight frame into the guesthouse, almost knocking me over. His cheeks were flamed over and his eyebrows were so fur-rowed together they looked almost like a unibrow.

"We need to talk to you right this minute, young lady!" my father barked. That's when I looked behind him and saw my mother standing there too. That wasn't a good sign—the two of them coming together to speak to me. I could tell that my mother had been crying. She had crumpled tissues in her hand and no makeup on. She never came outside, even to get her newspaper, without a face full of makeup. When I saw her, coupled with my father's raging look, I knew some shit was up. *Oh boy. What now?* I said in my head.

"Look at you! You can try to hide behind that robe all you want, your face tells it all. Mascara smeared all over your face . . . look at you! You've been partying again, right? You've clearly been drinking and you smell!" my father continued his tirade.

He was so close to my face that his breath was blowing straight up my nostrils and the stale cigar smell threatened to make me hurl. I stepped back from him and turned up my face in a rude display of disapproval. I rolled my eyes and flopped down in the recliner. I put my head down on the arm of the chair, letting them know I was not interested in the bullshit they were popping so early. I buried my nose in the arm of my robe and just listened to my father continue his rant. He was going on and on and I buried my face further and further. It was all I could do to keep from throwing up. My mother would chime in every so often.

Finally, I grew tired of them and lifted my head up a little bit. I was trying to keep it together, but I couldn't help but look at them like they were crazy. They never showed this much interest in me before. All of the questions they were throwing out there and all of the sudden parent concern was new to me. In fact, from the time I could remember, both of my parents were into their own worlds. They would take long, expensive trips and leave me with a nanny when I was younger. My mother would take me a few places here and there, but that wasn't until I was much older. They threw money at me to keep me happy but they didn't really spend that much time with me or tell me they loved me. I could never remember my parents taking me to birthday parties or family outings, aside from expensive trips, but even the nanny came on those and I would spend most of my time with her. My parents had fucking audacity. They didn't have grounds to question me! They had made me into the monster that I was, so in my mind . . . they were going to have to fucking deal with it.

"Explain this right now, Megan!" my father barked, shoving a stack of papers into my face. He had been yelling the whole time, something about my so-called reckless behavior and money mismanagement, blah, blah, blah. I hadn't been tuned in until he pushed those papers into my direct line of vision. I crinkled my face and recoiled like he had just put a pile of shit under my nose. I barely looked at the papers but I knew immediately what they were—his credit card statements.

I looked at him and them, still trying to seem uninterested.

So what! I was saying with the look on my face, but in my head I was saying, *Oh shit, he is clocking my spending.* My father had never complained before. He had always told me money was no object, so what the fuck was the problem now? I knew I had probably doubled or tripled my spending, but that was how I was raised . . . spending and throwing money away carelessly.

"This is more than just regular college girl shopping and spending, Megan!" my father screamed with more of a worried look on his face now than angry. "What are you doing out there? These bills are rolling in faster and faster and getting higher and higher from month to month. This is not normal at all, Megan. The accountant pointed out some things to me and I have questions! What is a girl your age doing charging expensive bottles of champagne at several different nightclubs? What are you even doing in nightclubs so often? And what are these hotel suites with room service? You live here in Virginia Beach in an estate almost as big as a hotel! You have your own space! More than some adults have and you need to charge luxury hotel suites? What are you doing? I want answers now, Megan!" he screamed. Blood had rushed into his entire face, casting him a deep red. I could see a large vein that showed up green against his light yellow skin, pulsating in his neck.

My heart was hammering in my chest but I didn't really know why. I couldn't say that I was scared of him at all. My father's bark was always worse than his bite. I had to admit though, this tirade seemed different, more serious than I've ever seen before. I still was going to hold on to my spoiled girl bit and act rude.

"So what. I stayed at a hotel with Krista. We partied a few

nights . . . so what! Were you around? No. You and Mom were off traveling or whatever old people do," I screamed rudely. I didn't care about having respect for them. I was telling straight lies and trying to flip the script right back on them. I was so used to manipulating them and throwing tantrums to back them off of me that it was now like a way of life for me. "Why all of the questions all of a sudden? Why do either of you even care?" I continued. My little tantrum didn't seem to sway either of them at all.

"You need to stop the lying, young lady," my mother interjected. "You have not seen Krista. You are lying so much that you don't even know that Krista is traveling around Europe for her last year in college. Not like you. You disgust me. All you want to do is spend money, party, and be a failure!" my mother screamed, tears rolling down her face like crazy. I rolled my eyes and sucked my teeth at her. She was making me want to jump up and curse her out. The nerve of her selfish ass. Who did she think taught me everything I knew?

"I don't have to lie! I wish both of you would just leave me alone!" I spat, covering my face to hide my tears. I knew they were right and just them being there had kind of touched me and caused me to cry. I wasn't going to let them see me cry though. Showing weakness wasn't a characteristic I was comfortable with.

I could hear my mother sobbing. To me that bitch was pathetic. If she hadn't always been so busy trying to keep my father from cheating with his little whores maybe she would have had time for me. Our little dysfunctional family! If my mother and I weren't getting plastic surgery or shopping for something for her to wear at one of their "exclusive events," my mother would never have spent a minute with me. Anything she did with or for anyone else had to benefit her. I was just like her and I was starting to hate her for it.

"Don't tell us you're not lying! You are definitely fucking lying, Megan Rich. Look at this bill. Look at the things my accountant highlighted. It was your card being used to buy these things. Men's clothing? For who? You even charged two men's thirty-five millimeter Rolex watches from Reed's Jewelers when we got on you for buying one two years ago! What are you doing out there, Megan! And why haven't I seen any grades since you say you went back to school? What the hell are you doing, little girl?" my father belted out. His face was as red as a cooked lobster and even more veins were visible now. I thought he looked like he was about to stroke out at any minute.

He had never checked my credit card statements line by line before. This was something out of the ordinary. That fucking accountant was so nosy. I suddenly felt hot all over my body. I felt like the world was closing in on me. My reckless behavior was catching up to me. I was craving for some ecstasy or purple haze at that moment. Even a bottle of Hennessy would've done the trick. Any kind of substance that would've taken me out of that moment. I wished Eric would swoop in and whisk me away right then. Or at least swoop in and give me some of the drugs he was always supplying me with.

"And where the hell is your car?" my mother asked out of nowhere. I wanted to tell her to shut the fuck up and mind her own business. I hated her even more now. We had grown farther and farther far apart in the two years since Eric and I had started dating. She had become like my archenemy because she was always acting suspicious of every little thing. She always had ulterior motives so I had to think about her actions for a minute. I had it all mapped out in my head within a few minutes. My mother was bringing the attention to me because she knew it would keep my father at home. He was always all about me and she knew it. I could remember so many times she used me to get my father to come home early from one of his many business trips. I truly believe I am the reason my father stuck around with her so long. My mother knew that bringing this stuff to my father's attention would make him worry about me so much that she would be able to keep him close to home a little more often and a little longer at a time.

They went on yelling for a few minutes, but nothing had prepared me for what my mother did next. She stalked over to an accent table that was near the wall by the front door of the guesthouse. My eyes grew wide and a cold sweat broke out on my forehead when I noticed where she was heading. I jumped up, but it was too late. My mother had yanked the drawers out of the accent piece and she began dumping the contents of the drawers onto the top of the table. Sure enough, out fell my stash.

"You think I didn't know about this? Ohhh yes! Martha found these! She told me all about it. Now why don't you explain this to your father!" my mother screamed. Her tears were all dried up. She was jutting her fingers toward me accusingly, complete with full dramatics. This entire confrontation was unfolding like some soap opera or a bad melodrama. My mother held the bag containing my shit up by her pointer and thumb and flicked it back and forth as she ranted out her findings. "What is it, Megan? Go ahead, tell your father! Tell him!" she ranted like a mad woman.

My father was staring at her quizzically. Then he looked at me. My face was beet red and I felt real dizzy.

"Go ahead, Megan . . . tell your father what this is," my mother demanded cruelly, with her eyes squinted into little dashes as she was still waving the evidence in front of her.

I remained silent. I guess my silence was sort of like an admission of guilt.

My father looked from my mother to me and back again. I didn't open my mouth. I was too stunned and too angry to answer her. My father walked over to my mother and snatched the package. He examined it closely and then looked over at me. I could've sworn I saw fire flashing in his eyes. Mixed with his anger was apparent hurt.

"Tell me this bag does not contain drugs, Megan," he said, seemingly fighting back tears. I just put my head down in shame. My BlackBerry started buzzing on the glass top coffee table and kind of startled everyone. It definitely was a welcome distraction. I looked at it and saw it was Eric. Now I was really feeling anxious. I knew if I didn't answer Eric's call he would disappear with my car for the rest of the day or even longer and shit would just get worse.

"Answer me, young lady!" my father boomed, rushing into me and grabbing my arm roughly. He caught me off guard because he had never put his hands on me in my life. I was truly shocked.

"Ouch! You're hurting me!" I squealed like a big baby. My father tightened his grip on my arm and squeezed harder. "Owww!" I hollered. I could feel the blood pooling in my arm and just knew I'd have the ugliest bruise after he loosened his grip.

"You answer me . . . answer me right now, Megan! Are you taking drugs?" my father huffed. Small drops of spit flew from his mouth and landed on my face. He was like a damn possessed demon. He tightened his grip even more when I didn't answer him. The pain was unbearable now.

"Get off me!" I screamed, trying to wrestle my arm from his painful grasp. He wasn't letting up. "It's not mine, okay?" I whined, letting the lie slip from my mouth as easy as the truth would've. I was squirming, trying to get away. "It's not mine, Daddy!" I cried in a baby voice. My father eased up his grip when I whined like I used to when I was a little girl. He was butter against the sun when it came to hurting me. I got free and moved far away from him.

"Megan . . . I'm . . ." my father started, his voice cracking. It was hard for me to see him so disappointed in me.

"What? You believe her, Gavin? These are drugs and they are hers! I had them tested. It is MDMA or ecstasy pills. C'mon, Gavin. Don't let her manipulate you right now!" my mother yelled. She was avoiding eye contact with me.

"Why don't you mind your business!" I screamed at her.

"This is my business! You show all of the signs of using drugs! I read up on it. Just look at those bags coming up under your eyes. All of the money you spend, dropping out of school, all of the secrecy, all of the lies. Megan, I know the truth even if your father is too naive to believe it!" she replied.

My father was shaking his head. He was caught in the middle, I could tell. I had put some doubt in his mind about the drugs, which was just what I had intended.

"Megan, I don't know if you're using those pills or not," my father started again.

"Oh my God, Gavin! So now I have to lie on my own child? Is that what you think of me? I have nothing better to do but to lie on your precious princess?" my mother interjected, her voice a shrill cacophony. I don't know who had hurt her more . . . me with my drug use or my father for not siding with her against me.

"Shut up, Priscilla! This is not about you! I am talking to Megan . . . my daughter. Give me a damn chance to handle this situation without any input from you! Letting you make decisions is why we are in the financial fix we're in!" my father retorted.

My mother's face changed. She had been shut down. I felt a slight sense of satisfaction too. I didn't know what financial fix my father was referring to, but I didn't care. I was still going to spend money just like I wanted to spend it. My father turned his attention back toward me. I was standing with my arms folded looking dead at my mother. If eyes could kill she would've dropped dead right then and there. She realized she was losing ground in her campaign to bring me down.

"Megan, I'm going to tell you this just one time. I am fed up with your partying and expensive spending habits. And if you're taking drugs you better stop it as of today. You have only one choice. Yes, this is a goddamn ultimatum. If you don't enroll back in school or find yourself a job, come work for the company, or do something I deem worthy, then your mother and I are going to cut you off financially. And I do mean *completely off* . . . no credit cards, daily cash, no new things, no vacations . . . nothing, Megan. When I cut you off and say I am done, there will be no turning back for you. No turning back," my father warned, his pointer finger extended out in front of him for emphasis.

His words stung like hard slaps to my face. In fact, I put my hand up and held my face like he had really slapped me. The tears came in uncontrollable streams now. I hated when my father was mad or disappointed in me. My mother looked on like she was very satisfied with what he had just said.

I didn't have anything to say to either of them. I snatched up my BlackBerry from the coffee table and stormed past my mother, bumping her shoulder as I went by. I went into the guesthouse master bedroom, slammed the door and locked it. I flopped down on the bed and buried my face into one of the pillows.

"Megan, this is your fair warning. If this all doesn't stop, you will be cut off!" my mother screamed from the other side of the door. I guess she thought she had to emphasize the point.

"Leave me alone!" I screamed in reply. I picked up my phone to dial Eric back. Little did I know those words I had just said, especially "alone," would surely come back to haunt the shit out of me.

3

My Rude Awakening

I guess you could say I didn't believe my father's threats the day he and my mother barged up in the guesthouse. In fact, I was daring them to go through with their threats. I was pushing the envelope in more than one way. That very same day, I pulled myself together, left the house, and met up with Eric. We went on yet another shopping spree. This one I did on purpose. I mean, who the fuck did my parents think they were throwing those threats around like that? During my and Eric's spree, I had purchased what had to be no less than eight pairs of Louboutins that I definitely didn't need. I already had a closet full of shoes. I bought two or three high-end pocketbooks, even though my bag collection was over the top and I didn't need another at all. I purchased a short mink jacket for Eric and two pairs of Gucci shoes. He also got a diamond-encrusted pinky ring and a diamond cross pendant that hung from a long platinum chain. We had literally shopped until we were dog tired. It was all out of spite too. I was basically saying fuck my parents and what they had to say.

I also ramped up my recreational drug use. I was still popping ex, but I had also moved past the purple haze and started giving all of my attention to my mother's prescription drug collection. I had Vicodin, Oxycontin, and Percocet to keep me high as a kite whenever I wanted. My mother had so many different legally controlled substances that she didn't even miss them. Eric had also showed me how to do lines of coke, but that shit had hurt my head for at least two days after I first did it, so I wasn't a big fan.

I kept doing my thing for another year at least. When I turned twenty-four, I noticed that my father didn't give me a gift. He was out of town on my birthday, something that he had never let happen in my entire life. My mother barely said happy birthday to me that day either. To fix them, I took a large lump sum of money out of the bank. When I had told the bank teller my withdrawal amount was going to be fifty thousand dollars, the woman looked at me like I was speaking the native language of the planet Mars. It had taken a long time and a slew of signatures before I was allowed to get the money. I had even been given a room in the back of the bank near the vaults so that the money could be counted in front of me. It was an exciting experience, I must say. I guess my father was used to shit like that. I knew then I could get used to that type of royal treatment as well.

When I walked out of the bank with that money, Eric was sitting in the Range waiting for me patiently. He was happier than a faggot with a bag of dicks. I liked making him happy but it was starting to wear on me. He was always so demanding and if I didn't have something to offer him, he would do shit like disappear for the day or act stink toward me. Most of the time his little antics worked to get me back on track handing over money or taking him shopping. There were a few times when he could tell I was slipping and I had gotten tired of him. Whenever Eric would see me slipping, he would offer me some type of substance of comfort. The day we went to the bank was the first day he gave me crystal, aka methamphetamine. I had heard it referred to as the housewife drug, but I didn't know what the hell that meant. I surely wasn't a housewife but my mother was. I wouldn't put it past her to have used crystal at some point. When Eric gave it to me, I had smoked it the first time, but Eric quickly showed me how to shoot it into my vein for a much quicker high.

Damn. There was nothing like that shit. I had taken enough recreational drugs to know the difference. Meth was hardcore and it made me forget everything. I got so fearless with my shit that I started boldly taking Eric to the guesthouse on my parents' estate. I didn't care anymore if my mother and father came back from one of their trips and saw him there. At that time I was clearly convinced that their threats and their ultimatums were baseless and full of shit. I will admit that I never believed that my father would follow through with his threats.

So what did I do? I continued on with my drug use, my absenteeism from home and definitely from school, not to mention my reckless spending sprees.

I remember my rude awakening as crystal clear as if it were happening all over again.

"Yo! Wake your fiend-ass up!" Eric had called out, shaking me roughly.

"Mmm," I groaned. One thing about using crystal meth

was it made me always want to either be high or in the damn bed.

"Yo! Megan, I said wake the fuck up! I need some cash and we need to go to the bank! Let's go!" Eric barked, slapping me hard on my bare legs. I rolled my eyes and buried my face into the pillow. He always needed more and more cash. That day it seemed to me like I had just turned over fifty grand to him the week prior. I mean I knew it had been a couple of months, but that wasn't a little bit of money either.

"I don't know if I can get any more right now. The last time I was home I overheard my father complaining to one of his business associates about the recession and things changing," I told Eric. It was true. My father had been acting as if he needed to scale back our spending. My mother had even stopped getting so much Botox and plastic surgery. My father seemed a bit more stressed out lately, but he had not said anything to me about it yet.

"Your father got money to fuckin' burn. You probably got a trust fund bigger than some banks. Get the fuck up and let's go. I need you to front me some cash for a re-up," he demanded. Then he threw a small pack of meth at me.

I was up after that. I grabbed the bundle and padded into the bathroom to get off. When I stepped up to the hotel sink, I noticed how fucked up I looked. My hair was in desperate need of a wash and set, which I used to get every other day but hadn't had in over a month now. I looked down at my nails; they were chipped and the nail polish was a mess. This was all uncharacteristic of my usual. "Ugh, I look like a fuckin' mess. Pull yourself together and stop this shit, Megan," I said to myself.

When Eric and I pulled up at the bank, I had to cover my eyes with a pair of out of season Gucci shades. Damn, that wasn't like me either. I usually stayed on top of my fashion game and would have the very latest of everything. I walked into the bank and went to the familiar teller, the one I had used before to take out large sums of money. The woman smiled at me like she'd known me my entire life. I just nodded and smirked. I knew she was being phony because she and I both knew I was looking terrible compared to the last time she saw me.

I filled out the withdrawal slip and gave her my identification, although I know she knew who I was. She looked down at the amount, twenty thousand, and she didn't even flinch. She just kept that phony ass smile plastered to her heavily made-up face. I guess she was used to me by now. The woman began pecking on the computer keyboard as I tapped my foot waiting.

I wanted to get high again and I planned on taking some of the money for myself before I handed most of it over to Eric. I was kind of tired of Eric piecing my shit out to me like he pleased. He said he did that to keep me from getting addicted, but I think it was too late for that now.

The teller looked up at me with a serious, even ominous look on her face.

"Um . . . Ms. Rich, are you sure this is the account you want to use?" the woman asked nervously. Her smile had faded.

I pulled my shades down a little bit on my nose and looked at her over the top of them. "What? Isn't that the account I always use?" I asked impatiently.

"Yes, ma'am, but this account has been frozen. I am unable to process your transaction at this time," the woman said.

My face must've told her what I was thinking. She didn't give me a chance to open my mouth before she began to explain. "It has a note here saying the main account holder, a Mr. Gavin Rich, has frozen the assets in this account and will come into the bank to liquidate the account and close it. No funds are to be released from this account. I cannot even give you an account balance. I am afraid you have been shut out of this account, Ms. Rich. . . . I am very sorry," the woman rambled.

My body was hot all over with anger. My heart raced inside my chest and my stomach churned. I wanted to just melt away, but I had no choice but to stand my ground. "Is there another account I can use? I mean, what am I supposed to do for cash?" I asked, my voice cracking. The woman was looking at me sympathetically, which just made me even angrier. I wasn't a goddamn charity case like she was making me out to be.

"I'm sorry, ma'am. All of Mr. Rich's other accounts are single owner or joint with another party. There are no other accounts that contain your name. You are not authorized to receive funds from any other account. I am so sorry, Ms. Rich," the woman said apologetically. I believed that she sincerely felt sorry for me.

"That's fuckin' impossible! My father wouldn't cut me off like that!" I screamed, hurt evident behind my words. Everybody in the bank turned to look at me. The woman began blinking rapidly. She was clearly nervous as hell.

"Get your fuckin' manager now!" I barked at the woman. I knew that the answer wasn't going to be any different from the manager, but I didn't know what else to do to quell the ache of embarrassment and hurt I was feeling.

The manager, a tall Hispanic man, came rushing over to me. "Ms. Rich, maybe we can go to the back and speak," he said calmly, with his hands up in a sign of surrender.

"I don't wanna go in the fucking back! I want to get my money out of the bank right now!" I screamed. I didn't even realize I was stomping my feet for emphasis.

The man was clearly trying to remain calm and to calm me down as well. "I'm afraid that your joint account holder has requested to take you off the account, ma'am. This is out of our control now. You will have to speak with him or her," the manager said curtly. Now he was growing irritated with me because we had drawn the attention of a crowd.

"Fuck you! Don't tell me who I need to speak to, you bastard! I will have you know that I am rich! My family has done business with this bank for years. I will have your job by tomorrow so you might as well quit right now! We won't be doing business with this piece of shit bank again!" I screamed as I stalked toward the door. The heat of what seemed to be a million gazes was burning a hole in every part of my body.

My words were a bunch of empty threats and I knew it. I knew the manager and the teller were only doing their jobs, but I couldn't control the sheer anger that had grown into a palpable ball inside me. I stomped toward my car and I could feel Eric's hard glare following me around the car through the windshield. The fallout from coming out of the bank empty handed was one I wasn't up for. Whenever I couldn't get Eric what he wanted, it was never a good outcome.

"What the fuck happened?" Eric asked before I could fully put my ass into the passenger seat of *my* car.

I just busted out crying as I slammed the door. I thought maybe my tears would soften the blow of what I was about to tell him. I thought maybe, just maybe, he would feel the least bit of sympathy for me.

"My fucking father froze my account! They wouldn't even let me get a dollar out of it! They said he took my name off, froze the money, and plans on liquidating it and closing it all together!" I relayed through tears. I covered my face with my hands.

"What the fuck am I supposed to do now, Megan?" Eric screamed, totally unsympathetic. I moved my hands from my eyes and looked over at him like he was crazy. No apology, no sympathy or empathy from Eric, just pure selfishness coming from his ass. He slammed his hands on the steering wheel and startled me.

I jumped and looked over at him. "Eric! Did you hear what I said? My father cut off my money! I don't fucking know what you're supposed to do!" I barked at him. My head was spinning. I wanted to go home. I wanted to see my father and beg for mercy. I wanted to say sorry, but I knew that wouldn't work at this point. I was feeling a nauseating rush of mixed emotions.

Eric started rubbing his chin like he was in deep thought. "What about your credit cards? Can you get a cash advance off those?" Eric asked frantically, like he had come up with the next great idea or invention.

I was shaking my head from left to right. I couldn't believe him. "I can try," I mumbled, defeated.

Eric wasn't going to let this slide. He would hound me until he got what he wanted. "How much can you get from each card?" he asked.

My shoulders slumped in defeat and I just threw my hands up "I don't know. . . . I've never had to take a cash advance from a credit card," I said honestly. I had never been in this position before. No cash on hand and no access to any. It was a new low for me.

Eric whipped the car from in front of the bank. "Call your credit cards and find out—now," he demanded.

I called the customer service lines for all ten of the credit cards I had in my wallet and once again I was defeated. My father had closed every single credit card account that I had. I don't think anything except a dagger to the heart could've hurt more than finding out that my father had actually cut me off. I didn't think it could get any worse.

"Eric, I need to go home. I need to see my father and talk to him in person. I have to do it alone," I cried. I dropped Eric off back in his hood and drove straight home. I needed for my father to tell me in person that he had definitely cut me off for good.

I raced into the house and straight to my father's office. I was frantic. He wasn't there. I went to the main living room and that is where I found him and my mother. They were sitting together sipping champagne as if they didn't have a care in the world. Neither of them looked like they had a problem with cutting me off, nor did they appear as if they were waiting for me. I knew I looked bad so I stopped walking fast when I noticed them and I used my hands to try and smooth back my hair and make sure my face was clean. I licked my ashy lips and continued to try and spruce myself up as I walked into the living room slowly. I was trying to will myself to remain calm. I kept telling myself that there was probably a perfectly good explanation for what had been done. Maybe my father had changed banks and just hadn't had the chance to tell me. Maybe he had opened a bigger and even better bank account for his baby girl and was dying to give me access. I forced these thoughts into my head to keep from going crazy on their asses. I didn't want to believe that he had just left me out there for dead with no money.

My father was the one who noticed me first. He stood up and placed his champagne glass on the small table that sat between my mother and him. He had a halfhearted smile on his face and he quickly shoved his hands down into his pockets. That was not his typical greeting for me. There would be none of his usual open-armed embraces.

"Megan. What a nice surprise. Are you all right?" my father asked in a nice, calm voice like it was a regular day and we were seeing each other under regular circumstances. "You want to join us for snacks?" he asked, turning his body slightly to show me the table that had the champagne, orange juice, and homemade tea biscuits and pastries on it.

His smug tone made a flash of heat come over me. I couldn't understand why his ass was acting as if he had not done anything. My eyes were squinted into little dashes and I used the back of my hand to wipe my running nose . . . another downside to that meth shit. I walked toward my father and finally I opened my mouth. "No! I'm not all right! I didn't come here to eat your fucking pastries either! What did you do, Daddy? I can't get any money at the bank! I have nothing! What did you do?" I screeched, and I immediately lost control. There went the tears and wracking sobs. I was devastated by what I figured as his ultimate betrayal.

"I did what I told you I would do a year ago if you did not straighten up your life. I cannot condone your behavior as of late and I certainly cannot afford it," he chastised.

My mother stood up and wrapped her arms around the front of her. She started hugging herself as if she was very cold. She seemed as if this was hurting her when I knew fucking better. It was all a concerned mother act coming from her.

"So how am I supposed to live, Daddy? How am I supposed to take care of myself? Just like that you leave me with nothing. . . . I can't even buy a cup of coffee," I screamed through tears. Snot and tears covered my face now. I had taken off my shades to reveal eyes that were rimmed with bags.

"Megan, over the past year you should have thought about all of that. You had more than enough money and chances to buy coffee. Look at you . . . You are a mess. I have talked to Dr. Klusky and he gave me some literature about drug abuse. I can see the signs, Megan. Your mother and I think that you need to go to rehab. If you want to get help, I will pay for it and if you complete it we can try to start over. I will be here for you if you agree to get the help that you need. If you refuse the help, not only will you remain financially cut off, you will have to leave this house and the guesthouse. You will not be allowed onto this estate. You need to make a decision now. I will not give you any more time to think about this," my father said harshly.

I doubled over and dropped down to my knees. I could not fucking believe my ears. I was overwhelmed with wracking sobs.

I was devastated, to say the least. "I don't need rehab! You and your fucking quack doctor don't know what you're talking about," I screamed angrily.

"Megan, you will stop using that language in this house. You know your choices," my father said, flopping back down in his chair. He looked like this was just as painful for him as it was for me.

I noticed his face softening and took that as my chance to appeal to his softer side. "Please don't do this, Daddy! I don't need help. I swear I am not using drugs. I drink every now and then, but I swear to you, I am fine. I promise. Daddy, please don't do this to me. I will go back to school. I will work for you. I will do anything it takes to make this better," I pleaded through sobs.

"Megan, you are pathetic. Your father has given you our stipulations and they are final," my mother said dryly, finally speaking up.

I looked at her with hate-filled eyes. "I hate you! You were always jealous of me! I know this is all your doing!" I screamed at her.

"I will not have you speak to your mother that way. You will need to leave. Martha and the help have packed up your things and I will have them delivered to whatever address you'd like. You can keep your car . . . it is still yours," my father said cruelly. Every time he said anything I felt another pang of hurt. I was screaming and crying. I was a mess.

"I can't watch this anymore. I am going upstairs," my mother said.

"Megan, are you going to take my offer of rehabilitation or will you choose to leave this house?" he asked.

"I don't need rehabilitation! I don't need you either! I don't need any of you! I will show you! I can make it out there on my own! You made me into this monster and now you just toss me away like a piece of trash! I hate both of you!" I wailed. I pulled myself up off the floor and stood toe to toe with my father.

"I hope you are satisfied with what you have done to me. This was all your fault," I said indignantly. My father just looked at me pitifully. I turned around and stormed through the house. When I made it to the foyer I noticed my mother's pocketbook. I grabbed it and hurried out of the house. It was the last time I'd be home in a long, long time.

4

My Dose of Harsh Reality

To say that I was devastated by my father's actions would be an understatement. I couldn't find the words to describe my feelings as I left the house I had grown up in for the last time. I had been turned out onto the streets by the very people who were supposed to protect me from the world. I was feeling dejected and revengeful. I wanted to hurt my parents as much as they had hurt me. As I stormed out of the house, I didn't leave before I got my hands on my mother's purse, which had about a thousand dollars in cash in it and her American Express card. I was so angry that day that taking my mother's shit was my way of having the last laugh.

What I did afterward was get with Eric and we used my mother's card to shop and buy things he could resell for cash. We were able to net about five thousand dollars worth of stuff before we walked into Saks Fifth Avenue. But we had to high-tail it the fuck out of there because my mother had reported her credit card stolen by the time we had gotten to Saks. Eric was the one who had enough street smarts to notice how the counter girl was trying to stall us there while her manager got the police on the line. Eric had been looking around at all of the stares coming from some of the store associates. He told me later that he knew right away that they were calling the cops and just trying to keep us there. I remember Eric leaning into me and saying, "We need to get the fuck out of here right now." I was so high and so naive to stuff like that, that I had laughed it off. Eric grabbed me by the arm and practically dragged me out of the store.

"Wait, I have to get my card back!" I had shouted. I was so stupid and it wasn't even my damn card.

"Shut the fuck up and run!" Eric belted out, and he took off. I followed suit and it was a good thing I did. We had gotten out of the mall parking lot just in the nick of time. I was in tears when Eric explained to me what had really happened. My parents were actually playing hardball for real. They had completely shut me out and cut me off. The fact that the store clerks were going to call the police on me could only mean that my mother had found out I took her money and her card and she had reported me.

With no money and no credit cards, I was forced to move in with Eric. Talk about culture shock. I was used to living in Crystal Lake Estates, where there were estates with gates and circular driveways. Eric lived in South Norfolk, basically the hood. He lived in an apartment complex that had doors so close to one another it reminded me of a seedy motel that I had seen on television. I had never even been to an apartment complex. Growing up, all of our family friends and all of my high school friends lived on estates. When Eric opened up his apartment door and I stepped inside, naturally my facial expression told it all.

"It ain't the palace you used to living in, hmm?" Eric said with an attitude, and he left me standing in the middle of the floor.

I didn't mean to make him feel bad, but looking around I knew it would take me some getting used to. Eric's spot was very small, but I must admit it was neat and clean. It was still not what I was used to. I could see every room in Eric's apartment if I stood in the middle of his living room. His couch was a worn leather piece that looked like someone had sliced it with a razor in some spots, and the recliner was a mismatch plaid material piece that looked like it had been gutted, with cotton spilling out of it in the middle. The coffee table looked like a throwback from the seventies and like it had been used as a butcher's block with so many nicks and scratches on it. I had never thought people lived like that in real life. I had only ever seen stuff like that in some of the movies or TV shows I watched.

Eric and I had frequented so many upscale hotels and I had lived in the lap of luxury so long that I never really thought about how he lived every day. Looking around at his raggedy furniture and shabby living conditions kind of confused me too. I was just wondering how someone like Eric, who always donned the best of everything, lived there. Eric wore the best clothes, either from hustling or that he got from me. He wore Rolex watches and thousands of dollars worth of jewelry, so I could not understand why he lived in a place like this. His bedroom looked even worse than any other place in the house. His bed was simply a mattress on the floor. No box spring, no bed frame, no bed skirt, no bunch of luxurious pillows, and certainly no regal headboard like I was accustomed to.

"You gonna have to get used to this shit here, rich girl," Eric had announced the first day I came to stay.

I had tried to smile and act as if it would be fine with me, but I don't think he bought the fake smile on my face. He kind of had an attitude that entire day.

"I know it's not what you're used to, but I guess it beats being homeless," Eric had followed up.

I definitely couldn't bring all of my clothes to his house. My walk-in closets were bigger than his entire place, so I had only taken a few things with me; even what I considered just a few things was still too much for the closet he called an apartment.

After looking around, I had starting thinking that maybe rehab didn't sound so bad, but there was no way I could ever go groveling back to my parents. I was way too angry at them. The first two weeks at Eric's house I was fine. I had made myself get used to the cramped quarters and the horrible furniture. I stayed high enough to escape reality and Eric laid the dick down on me enough to satisfy any doubts I had about remaining in a relationship with him. I had not heard from my parents and soon found out that they had even cut my cell phone service off. I thought that was as petty and as low as they could go. It sent the message that they obviously didn't want to stay in touch with me. . . . How fucking worried could they be? They knew I didn't have any money and they didn't care where I was living or anything. Fuck them!

It was about the third week that I was with Eric that shit

started going downhill fast. Eric had been out hustling, or "working" as he referred to it, and I was at home. He had my car so I was stuck. Besides, not being from Norfolk, I was too scared to venture out alone. I had woken up one morning and looked over at the cable box, which like the bed, also sat on the floor. The box read 7:18. I sat up and looked around. I quickly realized that Eric was not in the bed, nor had he ever been the night before. Then I remembered finally falling off to sleep waiting for him and, with no way to contact him or question him about his whereabouts, I wasn't left with many options.

I got out of the bed and walked into the living room. Eric wasn't out there either and I had already passed the bathroom door so I knew he wasn't in there. It was finally clear to me that Eric had not come home. My heart sank as I flopped down on his beat-up sofa. The cracked leather pricked my bare legs and sent a sharp dose of reality through my psyche. Not only wasn't Eric at home, but he had not left me anything to get me high, which meant I would be dealing with being withdrawal sick in a few hours. I put my head in my hands and began to sob. I was all alone with no money, no parents, and no drugs. This would definitely be a harsh dose of reality for me.

I waited three hours before Eric finally put his key in the door and came into the apartment. I jumped up with a fire burning inside me that I had never felt. I rushed over to him before he could even make it all the way in the apartment and I began slapping and punching him. It felt like I was possessed. I was feeling a crazy adrenaline rush, which had given me a false sense of courage.

"I hate you! I hate you! I hate you!" I screamed over and over again while letting off a barrage of hits.

Eric was shocked and caught off guard. He grabbed my wrists tightly and pushed me off him. His face was drawn into a scowl. I didn't even care. I kept trying to get at him.

"What the fuck is wrong with you, Megan! You done lost your fucking mind or what?" he barked as he pushed me with enough strength to send me to the floor.

My body felt like it was melting. I felt like I wanted to curl up and die.

"Why didn't you come home, Eric? How could you leave me all alone with no money, no phone, no shit? After all I have done for you!" I wailed, kicking my feet and flailing my arms like a big baby. I was so used to throwing tantrums like this with my parents, I guess I thought it would work on Eric too.

"What? Don't be fuckin' questioning me. Look, I ain't ya daddy! I ain't responsible for your every fuckin' need! Maybe you need to get the fuck up and get a job! If not you need to come up with a plan to get some fuckin' money!" Eric screamed at me harshly.

My heart was breaking and it hammered painfully against my sternum. His words stung. After all I had done for him. All of the tons of money, the crazy high-priced gifts, the royal treatment he received during those expensive nights at hotels, and he had the nerve to turn around and tell me I needed to get a job. I was floored. I guess since I didn't have the money to splurge on lavish things for him anymore, Eric had grown tired of me just that fast. But he was all I had right now.

"Eric, please. I love you," I pleaded, quickly changing my

tone and my mood. I wanted to make up with him. I hated fighting with him. Besides, I needed him right now.

"You don't love me, Megan. You love what I represent, which is the very opposite of what you were. You wanted to be with me so you could have a little adventure on the hood side. You wanted some bad boy dick, so don't think you can convince me that you love a niggah. You are a selfish little spoiled rich girl. . . . Oops, I mean, you were a rich girl. I guess your parents showed you . . . huh?" Eric said cruelly. Then he walked into the bedroom and slammed the door.

He had left me on the couch looking stupid. I broke down again. I was distraught by his actions and his words. Maybe he was right. Maybe all I loved was his bad boy image. I started feeling overwhelmingly anxious. I couldn't let Eric slip away from me. I needed to show him that what he had with me was still perfect even if we didn't have a lot of money. At that point, I would've done anything to please him. Anything to get more money to make him happy. . . . Money was what made him happy and what would keep him with me.

5

My Desperation

Things with Eric just got worse with each passing day. He was verbally abusive and borderline physically abusive. He had already left bruises on my arms from grabbing me when he was frustrated with me a few times. He was not the same guy I had fallen for, that was for sure. Every day he took a new opportunity to tell me how worthless I was to him since I didn't have any money. The one thing he didn't fail to do was keep me high. I actually waited each day for Eric to bring me my fix like a dog waits for his master to feed him. Eric knew how to exercise control over me, but I could tell he was growing tired of me not having money or gifts to offer him. He would flip-flop between treating me like shit and treating me nice, usually for sex.

But as with everything, all good things eventually come to an end.

I was roused from my doped up sleep one morning by noise and voices coming from the living room. The apartment was so damn small there was no hiding the sounds. I lifted up my head to listen. At first, I thought Eric was on the phone with someone because I definitely recognized his deep baritone, but after listening for a few minutes, I could tell he was not alone. I sat up on the mattress and listened carefully.

"What the fuck is this niggah doing?" I whispered under my breath as I flicked off the covers and searched around for something to put on. I threw on some of my old Juicy sweat pants and one of Eric's T-shirts. As I rushed to get dressed, I clearly deciphered the sounds coming from the living room. It was that motherfucker Eric speaking to a female in the living room. He had actually had the elephant balls to bring a bitch to the apartment where I now lived with him. I was instantly sick of Eric's blatant disrespect.

I stormed out of the bedroom and rushed into the living room to find Eric and the bitch cuddled up on the couch. I rushed over to them and Eric didn't even flinch. He was sipping on a Bud and his eyes were lazy like he was high off his usual weed/cocaine mix. The girl looked like she was high too. She wore a lazy grin as well. She smiled at me like she knew me.

"W'sup, fiend? You up early. I didn't think I would see you until this afternoon," Eric said snidely, smiling at me too. I immediately felt like shit. He had referred to me as "fiend." I guess that is exactly what he thought of me now too.

"Ashley, this is Megan. . . . Megan . . . Ashley." Eric introduced us like it was nothing. He acted like I was his sister or just his home girl. I stood in jaw-dropping shock at Eric's brash audacity.

"Hi, Megan . . . I've heard a lot about you," Ashley said, then she busted out laughing and so did Eric. *What the fuck is so funny!* I screamed inside my head. I couldn't even speak. I looked at the girl and instantly felt like a piece of trash. She reminded me of how I used to look—beautiful, with everything seemingly flawless. Everything she wore was evidently expensive. She glistened with diamond jewelry and I saw her Gucci bag thrown on the coffee table. Ashley was very pretty in the face. She had what Eric liked to refer to as an "exotic look." Ashley had a caramel complexion, a very short, neat tapered hair cut, and from what I could see of her cleavage, she had a flawless body. Her nails were freshly manicured, eyebrows arched perfectly, and I could tell she had veneers on her teeth and thought maybe she had had a nose job. Eric had gone and found him somebody else to trick on his ass. It was clear to me that Ashley had money, which I knew she damn sure wasn't getting from Eric's leeching ass.

"Why she standing there like she saw a ghost?" Ashley said in a giggly, valley girl voice. Eric sure knew how to pick us. I could actually feel my blood boiling in my veins and suddenly I was spurned into action. It was like some unknown force was pushing me forward and controlling my every move.

"Eric, what the fuck are you doing? You bringing bitches home to our house now? Arggghhh!" I screamed, lunging straight for him.

Eric dropped his Bud, sending it to the floor with a crash. Ashley let out a scream and jumped up. I started scratching and slapping Eric in his face. He couldn't get to my hands because they were moving too fast. I could feel that I had drawn blood with my nails across his face.

"Owww, you bitch!" Eric barked.

"Oh, this bitch is crazy!" I heard Ashley say, then she

jumped on me. She punched me in the back of my head to get me off Eric. I turned my attention toward her, but not before she yanked my long hair and wound it up in her hand.

Ashley didn't have any hair for me to grab, so I had to rely on fighting skills. I had never had a catfight before, but Ashley clearly had. She was getting the best of me. She punched me dead in my nose and I felt the hot blood trickle out of my nostril and down my lips.

"Get off me, you bitch!" I wailed. Ashley punched me again. I was flailing my arms wildly but I wasn't hitting her at all. She hit me again with enough force to cause me to see little stars behind my eyes. "Aggh!" I screeched, and I continued to struggle to fight her. I finally got in a good swipe at her face, which caused her to scream.

"This bitch scratched my flawless face!" Ashley belted out. That caused her to let go of me. "You jealous bitch, you really scratched my face," Ashley screamed after she touched her face and noticed blood on her hands.

"Yo, Megan! What the fuck is wrong with you, you junky bitch! Get the fuck out of my house!" Eric boomed. He walked over to me. I didn't know what to expect so I threw my hands up in defense. Eric picked me up and slung me over his shoulder like a rag doll.

"Eric, please!" I screamed. He didn't say anything. He just started heading for the door. I was kicking and punching him in the back. "Agggh! Let me down! Eric! How could you do this to me? After all I did for you! I gave up my family for you! You motherfucker!" I cried at the top of my lungs.

Eric opened the apartment door and dumped me outside

on the ground. I landed hard on my knees and it hurt like hell. Nothing hurt more than what Eric was doing to me.

"Get the fuck from around here before you get yourself fucked up! You ain't got shit to offer and I'm tired of feeding you and your habits! When you find some fuckin' money, then maybe I'll consider taking your junky ass back!" Eric screamed at me.

"Please, Eric, don't do this!" I cried desperately.

"Get the fuck from around here!" he yelled at me. Then he picked up his foot and kicked me in my ass like I was a dog in the street. I fell flat onto my stomach from his kick.

"Ahhhh!" I cried. I couldn't even feel the pain of hitting the concrete with a thud. Eric's actions hurt me more than any physical pain I could've felt. I had never experienced a pain in my heart like that. I was completely devastated by his treatment. Eric's rejection hurt even more than when my parents had cut me off and kicked me out of the house. I couldn't move. Eric spit on the ground next to me and stalked back to the apartment door and slammed it.

The sound of the door closing sent a cold chill through my entire body. I was desperate now. I had to think of a way to get some money so that I could get Eric back. I was determined that Ashley wasn't going to have my man. I would make things right like they were when Eric and I had first met.

I stood outside the apartment for almost three hours. Eric and Ashley never emerged. I looked down from the tier into the courtyard on the other side of the complex and noticed a girl sitting on a car talking on her cell phone. I walked over to the courtyard, away from Eric's apartment building, and approached the teenage girl. I asked the girl if I could make a call on her cell phone. She looked at me like I was crazy at first. My appearance and my request had probably thrown her for a loop. Thinking fast and knowing that in the hood there always had to be something for something, I promised to give the teenage girl one of the many Gucci bags I owned in exchange for just one call. The little girl was hesitant at first. She eyed me suspiciously and I knew she was thinking that I looked like a damn mess and probably didn't own a Gucci bag.

I told her that I was Eric's girlfriend and she eased up and let me use her phone. It was a good thing everybody in the hood either knew Eric personally or knew of him. When the girl handed me her phone, my hands were trembling uncontrollably. It was a mixture of nerves and withdrawal setting in. I hurriedly dialed the familiar phone number and just prayed that my father would pick up.

After what Eric had done, I decided I was ready to go back home. I would do anything my parents asked me to do in order to get back home . . . even go to their stupid rehab program.

The phone started ringing on the other end. My teeth were chattering as I waited with the phone pressed tightly to my ear. My heartbeat automatically sped up with every ring. I started shifting my weight from one foot to the other. After the third ring with no answer a hot feeling of nausea came over me. My stomach began cramping.

"C'mon, Daddy, pick up," I mumbled through tears, biting into my bottom lip. I had started to lose my composure all over again.

Reality was setting in fast.

After about the fifth ring my father's voice mail came on. "Hi, you've reached Gavin Rich. I am currently out of the country for three weeks. I will return on the seventeenth. If you leave me a message, I will call you back upon my return. Thank you."

My heart sank and my shoulders slumped down in defeat. "What is today's date?" I asked the little girl.

She looked at me with a mean mug and smacked her lips. "Today is the fifteenth," she grumbled, her mouth curled at the ends. Then she gave me a look like "bitch, give me my phone." I still had two days to wait for my father to return. There was no way I could survive out on the streets for two days without Eric.

"Can I just make one more call, sweetie? I can make sure you are compensated," I pleaded with the little girl. She rolled her eyes at me. I knew with my hair sticking up, blood all over my shirt and my eye starting to swell, I probably looked like a crazy person or a crack fiend to the little girl. I was praying she didn't just snatch her phone and leave me hanging.

"Hurry up. I'm expecting some important text messages to come through," the little girl snapped, folding her arms across her chest. I didn't care if she was playing hardball with a nasty attitude, I was just grateful she was allowing me to use her phone. I quickly dialed my mother's number. It went straight to voice mail. I knew that meant she was probably with my father out of the country.

"Fuck!" I screamed, and the tears started streaming again. I really didn't have any place to go now. I handed the little girl back her phone and started walking up the street. I didn't know what I would do next. My mind raced with possible ways to get my hands on some money. That was the only way to please Eric at this point. I finally walked back to the apartment complex. I noticed that my Range was gone. That bastard threw me on the streets but had the nerve to still be driving around in my car. I decided I would sit in front of the apartment door and wait it out. I hoped and prayed that I didn't have to wait outside all night long. This part of town was no place for me to be standing around alone. But I figured that since I was, I might as well utilize the time to come up with an idea for Eric and me to get our hands on some money.

6

My Master Plan

Eric returned to the apartment early the next morning. I had been sitting outside by the door all night. He had never even given me a key to his place. I was also too stupid to ever request one from him. Over the course of the night, I had gone through several bouts of wracking sobs that would subside and turn into an overwhelming anger. When Eric finally decided to come home and walked up to the door, I had my head down on my knees. I looked up at him with pleading, red-rimmed, swollen eyes.

"Megan, I thought I told you to get the fuck from 'round here. If you want your car, here," Eric said, dropping my car keys next to me. He was so fucking cruel it wasn't even funny. I had tears in my eyes. The mere sight of him brought them on.

"Eric, I just want to be with you. I'm sorry I got so mad and attacked you. I can't deal with knowing you want to be with someone other than me. I love you, Eric," I cried, my words barely understandable through the sobs.

"I'm a grown-ass man and I gotta do what I gotta do to survive. I'm here feeding you and feeding your fuckin' habit," Eric snapped. He wasn't going to be nice for shit.

I had to just accept it if I wanted to get back into his good graces. He opened the apartment door with his keys. I stood there, my body stiff and rigid. I was afraid to just try to walk inside. I couldn't take any more blatant rejection from Eric.

"I have a plan to get some money . . . a lot of money," I blurted out. The words sounded desperate and shaky when they left my mouth. I just hoped that he'd stand around long enough to hear what I had to say.

"Come inside, Megan. You know damn well I wasn't going to leave you standing outside," Eric said, stepping inside first. Chivalry was never his strong point.

We went inside together. I stood near the door, uncomfortable. I didn't want to assume anything. I was going to wait for him to invite me all the way inside.

"Look at you. You sure don't look like the rich glamour girl you was when I first met you," Eric said as he walked over to me.

I swiped roughly at the tears threatening to fall again. I wanted to be strong, stand my ground. I didn't want him to think I was some little weak rich girl, when that is exactly what I was.

Eric grabbed my hand and pulled me into him. At first I kept my body stiff and erect, afraid to return his embrace. He hugged me tightly. "Relax. I'm not going to hurt you anymore," he whispered into my ear. With that my body went slack with a sense of relief. I melted into his embrace and began to cry again. "I didn't mean to hurt you, Megan. You just got me so fed. A niggah is hard pressed right now and that chick Ashley was giving up cash . . . the same cash that I use to take care of us. That's all it was," Eric said, stroking my tangled bird's nest of hair.

I knew Eric would never really hurt me. I knew there was a perfectly good explanation about why he acted out like that. I was so glad I didn't go running back home. I just wanted to be with him. "I'm sorry too. I didn't mean to attack you," I sniffled.

Eric lifted my chin with his hand and he kissed me. I closed my eyes and relished the moment. It felt so good. I opened my mouth slightly and accepted his tongue. We kissed so passionately that I instantly became wet. I could feel Eric's dick pressing hard into me through his clothes. Eric started breathing hard and removing my clothes. I was kind of embarrassed by how dirty I was from being outside. Eric didn't seem to care at that moment. He slid my sweatpants over my hips.

"Oh God, I never want to be away from you again," I huffed, my breath hot on his ear.

Eric pushed me down onto the coffee table. He dropped down and pulled his dick from his boxers. I closed my eyes in anticipation of what was to come. I was in heaven with my man again. Eric mounted me and drove his dick into my pussy so hard I yelped.

"Oww! Oh, Eric . . . yes, fuck me, please. I need you. I want you," I panted as I grinded my hips into him. I wanted him to stay inside me forever.

Eric slammed into my pelvis with brute force. He was fucking the shit out of me and I was loving every minute of it. I felt like I had him back. Eric was mine again. I was so in love.

Eric pulled me up off the coffee table and threw me down on the couch. He mounted me again and fucked me some more. This time he took my soaking wet pussy from the back. His skin slapping against my ass made a loud noise that drove me wild.

"Uhh! Yeah, Daddy, fuck me," I grunted.

Eric did just that. He fucked the shit out of me until I was screaming with an orgasm. Eric followed me with a big load of cum in my ass crack. I fell down onto the couch with my eyes closed. I was never so happy in my life. We lay on the couch together for a few minutes in silence. But the silence was short lived. Eric was the one who broke the silence. He broke up our moment.

"So, what's your plan to get some money? Let me hear about it," Eric said as he stroked my hair.

My eyes popped open. Just that fast I had forgotten that I had told him that I had a plan to get money. My mind started racing. I inhaled deeply and exhaled. Damn. Just when I thought he was being nice to me just because he loved me as much as I loved him. I should've known that Eric only wanted to know how I could get him some money. No wonder he was being so nice, so fast.

"Well, I'm listening. You made it seem like you had something in mind earlier. . . . So what was it?" Eric urged, sounding a bit impatient.

I had to think quick on my feet and something that had been just a fleeting thought in my mind suddenly came rushing back.

"I was thinking that I can call my father . . ." I started, kind of stumbling over my words a bit.

"C'mon, Megan! Be for real!" Eric boomed immediately. He pulled his arm from under my head and began to sit up like he was going to leave. I grabbed on to him, but he tugged away. "Your father ain't giving you no fuckin' money. If he ain't come looking for your ass this long, can't you tell he don't give a fuck about you?" Eric added, cutting me off before I could even finish. His words hurt, as usual. I couldn't hold on to him.

"Wait. Just listen to me," I pleaded.

Eric had bolted upright and stood up from the couch like he was suddenly repulsed by me, or like he'd been suddenly bitten by a wild animal. "If you talkin' bullshit I ain't got no time for it," he replied in an annoyed tone of voice.

"We can get my father and hold him for ransom money. We can demand a million dollars from his accountant for his release. I know his accountant will pay it . . . so will my mother. A million dollars is nothing for them," I blurted out, rambling like a child. The idea sounded ridiculous to me after I said it. I just knew Eric would start cursing and screaming at me, calling me stupid and childish. He didn't. He was actually tuned in and attentive for once. I looked at him wide eyed, hoping he'd like the idea I'd come up with.

"Shit, that might not be a bad idea. We can use you to get him to meet you somewhere and I can have some of my little peeps snatch his ass up. Yo . . . that shit might not be a bad idea at all. I ain't never even gotta get my hands dirty if I let them lil' niggahs do all the work. You better be sure that the mothafuckin' accountant gonna pay up though," Eric said.

I could tell his mind was racing. I smiled. I was so happy to finally please him. "Yes. Yes, Eric, I am sure they will pay.

We don't have to hurt him at all. Just snatch him. Keep him blindfolded until we get the money. Once we get the money we can let him go without him ever having to get hurt. He will never know that it was us either," I replied, trying to sound excited. I wanted to make it clear to Eric that my father was not to be hurt. I was shocking myself with some of the things I was saying.

"You really think they just gon' hand over a million stacks just like that?" Eric asked skeptically. He was rubbing his chin, something he did when he was deep in thought.

"I know so. My mother will be so spooked she will call the accountant right away. We could probably get the money within a few hours," I assured him.

"Yo, rich girl, I didn't think you had that devious shit in you. I'm impressed," Eric said, smiling.

I was so happy to see him smiling. I started grinning from ear to ear. "I told you I would do anything for you, Eric. I love you so much. You were here for me even when my parents were not. I would do anything to keep you happy," I said, letting my voice take on a serious tone.

"That's good to know. So when we gonna do this?" Eric asked, tossing a pack of crystal at me.

The packet landed right in my hand. My heart jerked with excitement.

"My father comes back in less than forty-eight hours. When he gets back, I'll drive to his office and I will find out his new routine. If he thinks I wanna go begging back to them he will talk to me," I said, making up the plan as I went along. In the meantime, I was anxious to get into the bathroom and get high.

"Sounds good to me. I like a bitch that can come up with a master plan when her back is against the wall. Shit, it's a good thing I threw your ass out and made you think about things. You know where the fuck your bread is really buttered at, don't you?" Eric replied.

"I sure do, baby. I never doubted you for one minute. I know everything you do is for the both of us," I said. I would've agreed with whatever he had said just to go get high. Even though I thought what he had said was kind of fucked up and nasty, I would've never protested at that point. I guess Eric's constant cruel words couldn't be any more fucked up than the plan I had come up with against my own father. I didn't know if it was my addiction or my serious infatuation with Eric, but I was turning into someone I didn't even recognize myself. Gone was the little rich girl from Virginia Beach.

I could not control my hands from trembling and my teeth from chattering as I pulled up at my father's office. I purposely drove around the back and parked my car at his service entrance. Before I got out to walk back to the front doors, I looked at myself in my car's visor mirror. "Still not the greatest, but I guess I got no choice," I whispered as I examined myself. I looked like I had aged a couple of years since I'd been away from home. My hair was desperately in need of a good salon visit and my nails were horrible. I had put on some makeup to mask the remnants of the bruises that were on my face. I tried to make my face look as vibrant as I could with what I had. I had also washed my own hair and left it wet. It hung in long curly locks, which also helped to hide some of my facial flaws. I thought that I looked better than I had in the past couple of weeks when all I had been doing was getting high and fighting with Eric.

"Ok. You look fine, now go do this," I spoke out loud to myself. I inhaled and tried to get my nerves under wraps. The track phone Eric gave me rang and caused me to almost jump out of my skin. I sucked my teeth as I grabbed for it. He had already called me at least ten times on the way over to my father's office. *What the fuck does he want?*

"Hello," I whispered into the phone, my voice shaky and unstable. Although I was in the car alone, I still felt the need to be secretive and whisper. I peeped back in the rearview mirror and I knew Eric was in a vehicle close by watching me. I don't think he trusted me to go through with the plan.

"Why you just sitting there? Hurry the fuck up and go inside. Remember, get him to come outside . . . to the back of the building. That's where it's going down at. You hear me?" Eric instructed for the thousandth time. He was driving me fucking nuts.

"Okay. I got it," I said, annoyed. I didn't need him making me feel more on edge. This whole deed was bad enough in my book.

I finally got myself together and exited my Range on wobbly legs. I stopped for a minute to shake off the creeps I was feeling. Afterward, I took a deep breath and walked around the building and into my father's office space. When I entered, the first thing in my line of vision was a huge, poster-sized picture of me when I was about four years old. My father had never taken it down in all of these years. It instantly made me nostalgic. With the sound of the door opening, the front desk assistant looked up from whatever she was doing on the computer. A wide smile spread across her face.

"Megan! What a nice surprise," Ms. Everett, my father's longtime assistant sang. The ample-breasted woman stood up and opened her arms to give me a hug. I let a nervous smile spread across my face and stepped into her embrace. She smelled like cinnamon and biscuits. Her hug made me feel warm inside, I guess like a mother's hug would, but since my mother never hugged me I had to just imagine.

"Mmmm, your daddy talks about you all the time. You know he really misses you. He just wants you to be good. He wants the best for you, Megan," she told me as she held me tightly.

I could feel tears burning at the back of my eyes. I pulled away from her. I didn't want to cry, nor was I there for her advice. I cleared my throat. "I know he does, Ms. E. That is why I am here. I just want to do the right thing for a change," I lied. "Is he here?"

"Yes, baby. He is in his office. I won't let him know you're here. I think this will be a great surprise for him," Ms. Everett said, smiling.

I smiled back and headed to the back where my father's office was located. I could see as I walked the long hallway that his door was closed. That usually meant he was very busy working on a new deal to make more money or that he was stressed out about something with his business. I was hoping for all of our sakes he was behind closed doors brokering a new deal for more money.

I stood in front of his door for a few minutes before I got up the courage to turn the doorknob. *C'mon, Megan, don't get shook now. You got a job to do,* I pep talked myself. Finally I twisted the doorknob and pushed the door open.

My father was sitting at his desk leaning over a stack of papers. "Yvette, I am not taking any calls and I don't want any lunch," my father said dryly, without looking up. He thought I was Ms. Everett.

I swallowed hard. My bottom lip was trembling. I was paralyzed with fear for a few minutes.

"Close the door behind you," he barked out, still not looking up.

"Hi, Daddy," I said in an almost inaudible whisper. My father looked up. He pulled his reading glasses off and his face softened. He looked like he wanted to cry. I could tell he was at a loss for words.

"I missed you, Daddy," I said softly, my voice cracking.

My father stood up slowly. Still he didn't speak. He rushed over to me with an urgency that made me uneasy. My eyes grew wide. I didn't know what to expect. My father walked into me with all of his might and grabbed me in the tightest embrace I had ever felt from him in my entire life. He immediately started to sob. I had never in my life heard my father cry. It broke my heart into a million pieces. Doubt about what I was doing started creeping in.

"Oh, Megan, baby girl, I've been so worried about you. I thought you would at least call, or come back home by now," he cried into the top of my head.

I began to cry as well. I held on to my father like I never wanted to let him go. In my head I was telling myself to stay strong. Stay on course with the plan. Remember how he had hurt me.

"Let me look at you," he said, pulling me away from him. He held me by my shoulders and looked at me closely. "You look like you need to eat. You look tired too. Where have you been? Why haven't you called me?" My father shot off questions and statements like rapid fire. The worry was evident in the creases of his face. That kind of touched me too. I thought the entire time I was gone he and my mother hadn't even given me a second thought.

"You cut off my cell phone. I had no way to call you," I told him.

"No! I would never toss you out and cut off your cell phone. I just wanted to teach you a lesson, Megan. I never meant for you to be away this long," he said, swiping at a tear in his eye.

It must've been my bitch of a mother who had turned off my cell phone then. She probably never wanted me to come back. I guess since I was grown up she could no longer use me as leverage to keep my father around her.

"Sit down. Talk to me. Are you ready to get some help? You know, go to that rehab place and start your life right," my father rambled.

I guess he didn't know what else to say to me. Especially since it was glaringly obvious that I was on drugs now. But still, something about his questions sent a searing hot flash through my chest. He was still on that rehab bullshit. I had just returned and he was talking some shit. You would think he would ask me if I needed some fucking money or a hot meal or maybe a place to sleep. My feelings of guilt were quickly replaced with anger. I felt a new wind beneath my wings to go through with my plan.

"Yes, Daddy. That is why I'm here. I am ready to do what

it takes to get back in your good graces. I want to be your baby girl again," I said deceptively, using a babylike voice that I knew would tug at his heart strings. I deserved an academy award for this performance for sure.

"Oh, baby. I am so glad. We can call Dr. Klusky right now and get you into a place. I will take care of all of your needs . . . anything you want. No expense is too much for me to see you get well again," my father said. He was getting ready to reach for the phone.

"Wait!" I belted out nervously. I couldn't afford for him to speak with Dr. Klusky right now. It would just fuck everything up. "Daddy, before I go to rehab or do any of that, I want to go out with you. To lunch . . . Just me and you, alone to talk about things. I want to drive you to this place that I like near the beach. You know, a father and daughter sit-down. We finally need to just sit down and talk things through this time. It has been a while. I don't want to come back and then leave right away without first spending some time alone with you," I lied. I was laying it on thick.

My father's eyes were sad and I knew he was buying it. He swiped away another tear. *Enough already with the crocodile tears,* I said to myself. I was starting to feel angry again. It was like the feelings came in waves.

"Anything you want, Megan. I will do anything that you want," he replied, grabbing my hand and squeezing it. I cracked a phony smile and gently pulled my hand away from him. I was uncomfortable now.

"Can we go now? If you can't, I understand. I know you're always busy. I can just come back another time when you have time," I said manipulatively. I knew he wasn't going to chance me walking out the door again and not returning.

"No! I always have time for you," my father protested. He picked up his central telephone line. "Yvette, hold all of my calls for the rest of the day. If Priscilla calls, just tell her I stepped out to a business meeting. You don't need to mention that Megan was here just yet. I want to tell her face to face," my father instructed. He wouldn't take his eyes off me. He looked like he somehow didn't trust that I was really there or that I would really stay and not bolt out the door.

I cracked a halfhearted smile at him. This shit was getting unbearable now, all of the phony love antics. I wanted to hurry up and get this over with. I could feel that my high was wearing off and my nerves were starting to take over me. I needed to get my father to hurry up. He finally hung up the telephone after giving Ms. Everett more instructions.

"You ready, baby girl? I am all yours for the day. No business calls, no Priscilla, no nothing, just me and my baby girl . . . the love of my life," my father said, placing his arm around my shoulder.

"Yes, Daddy. I am as ready as I'll ever be," I replied with more fake-ass cheesy smiles.

We walked out of his office arm in arm. My father started heading for the front door. I stopped walking and pulled him a little bit.

"Oh, wait, Daddy. I parked at the back of the building. I didn't want Ms. E to see my car and alert you. I wanted to surprise you," I lied some more.

"How sweet of you, Megan. Okay, let's go through the back

door to your car. I finally get to ride and let my baby girl drive me around," he said, smiling proudly.

I just fell silent. We got to the back door and my legs started to feel weak. I didn't know if I could go through with the plan. Something deep inside me wanted to tell my father to stay in the building and save me from Eric. But the nagging yearning for meth that I was experiencing propelled me forward and gave me incentive to go through with my plan. Besides, I had assurances from Eric that nothing would happen to my father. We would just put a blindfold on him, request the money, pick it up, and then release him safe and sound.

My father yanked on the door and we stepped out into the sun. There was a black van blocking my car in. My father immediately noticed. He crumpled his face into a mean mug. "Who the hell is this parked back here on my private property?" my father complained.

"I know . . . they have me blocked in," I replied, feigning annoyance.

My father let my arm go and walked over to the van to investigate. He lifted his balled up fist to knock on the side of the black van, but before he could hit the van's sliding door, the door slid open real fast. My father jumped, and from where I stood, so did I.

The rest of the shit happened so damn fast it felt like I blinked and my father had disappeared into thin air. When the doors flew open someone placed a black bag over his head and they grabbed him and dragged him into the back of the van. I had heard a short attempt at a scream come from his mouth but nothing after that. I was biting down into my bottom lip so hard I had drawn blood.

The track phone rang in my pocket. I was snapped out of my trance. I grabbed the phone with shaking hands and placed it up to my ear.

"What the fuck you standing there looking stupid for? Get your ass in your car and drive to the spot I told you to go to . . . now!" Eric screamed in my ear.

The next thing I heard was a gunshot blast coming from inside the office. I jumped so hard a little bit of piss escaped from my bladder. That's when I saw one of Eric's little henchmen running out of the back door to another car. He was holding the surveillance videotape. I cupped my hand over my mouth. There was only one other person inside the office.

"Oh no!" I mumbled under my hand. They had killed Ms. Everett because she would be a witness. "Oh my God," I cried, and closed my eyes. My legs felt like they were made of lead. Eric did not tell me that he was going to kill Ms. Everett, or anyone for that matter.

I slowly got into my car. Once I was in the driver's seat, the reality of what I had just done hit me like a ton of bricks. I slammed my hands on the steering wheel. "Fuck! Why? I am so fucked up!" I screamed at myself. I had betrayed my own father and now an innocent woman was dead all because of me. And for what? For the likes of Eric Chambers, ex-convict, selfish, male, gold-digging piece of shit. I punched the steering wheel again. Then I put my head down on it and sobbed. The van had long since pulled off. I had just turned my father over to wolves. I had just become an accessory to murder as well. Any way this whole thing turned out, I would be guilty of something.

I finally put my car into drive and headed to the planned rendezvous spot. I prayed all the way there that God would forgive me for this, and most of all that my father would make it out of this shit alive and well. Even if they took my life in exchange for his.

7

My Worst Mistake

When I walked into the warehouse that Eric had chosen to hold my father in, I felt cold all over my body. I saw that they still had the bag over his head, secured around his neck with thick, silver duct tape. They also had his hands tied together in front of him and his ankles bound with the same type of tape. He lay on his side on the floor. He was shivering like he was either cold or very afraid. That shit broke my heart. My father was mumbling through the bag but I couldn't understand him. The sight of him bound up like an animal made me sick to my stomach, but I took comfort in the fact that he wasn't injured. I knew this was going to be over very soon.

When Eric noticed me standing in the room, he rushed over to me and grabbed me roughly by the arm. I was numb and emotionless at that point. I didn't even flinch or say ouch, I just let him wrangle me up like I was his child.

"What the fuck took you so long to get here?" Eric whispered harshly.

I wrestled my arm away from him and rolled my eyes. He had some fucking nerve questioning me. "You didn't say anything about murdering the assistant. You promised me nobody would get hurt," I gritted, standing up to Eric. I had my face drawn into a frown just like he did. I wanted him to see my dissatisfaction with his bullshit.

Eric pushed me backward out of the room where they were holding my father. He grabbed my face and squeezed it. "Now you listen to me, rich girl. Either you go along with this and save your father's life, or you watch him suffer and maybe die if I don't get what I want," he said through clenched teeth. "Now get on that fucking phone and call the people you need to call. If not, neither one of y'all will make it the fuck out of here alive," he continued, fire flashing in his eyes.

I followed Eric to a small room that had a little black device on a table with a telephone. "Use this to disguise your voice," he said, tossing the little speaker-looking device over to me.

My hands were trembling so bad I could barely figure out how to use the damn thing. It baffled me where Eric got all of this shit from—a warehouse type place, a voice disguiser. It was immediately apparent to me that he was working with somebody obviously more powerful than himself.

Finally, I connected the device to the phone and dialed my mother's cell phone number. When she picked up, I could hear distress in her voice. She must've known about my father's kidnapping and maybe even about Ms. Everett's senseless murder by then. "Hello," she said on the other end of the phone.

I opened my mouth but nothing came out. I wanted to curse her, tell her this was all her fault for what she had convinced my father to do to me. I wanted to just let loose on her, but I couldn't speak. I was completely at a loss for words, because I knew I had made the worst mistake ever.

"Hello!" my mother yelled again, this time with more urgency in her tone.

Eric snatched the phone from me and glared at me evilly. He pushed me aside forcefully. I guess I was of no use to him or anyone else for that matter. I was a useless piece of shit just like Eric had been telling me for the past couple of weeks. I put my head down on the table. I felt like I wanted to die.

"Hello, rich bitch," Eric snarled. I could hear my mother screaming for Eric to identify himself. "Don't worry about who this is, bitch. You see that dead black bitch in your husband's office? Well, take that as a sign of what's to come. We have your husband, and you and your accountant are the only ones who can save him. We want three million in cash . . . no later than tomorrow or he dies," Eric growled through the voice modulator.

I bolted upright in the chair. I looked at Eric like he was losing his fucking mind. That request wasn't what we had discussed. I knew better.

When Eric slammed the phone down I started in on him. "I thought we were asking for one million dollars! Three million is too much for them to get up in one day! My father doesn't keep that much money on hand. That kind of money he would have tied up in assets and investments. His regular bank accounts total up to about one million. That is why I gave you that number, Eric!" I yelled at him. I knew he had already crossed the line. He had not even warned my mother about the police or anything. Eric was botching the whole plan, starting with the stupid murder he had committed for no reason! He wasn't the smart street-savvy guy I took him to be. In fact, I was now convinced that he was just plain fucking stupid.

"Too fuckin' bad. Look around. You think I own a warehouse and voice machines? You don't think I gotta hit these niggahs off with loot for snatching ya pops up? I need money to pay for all of this shit too, Megan! Niggahs are officially on the payroll for this bullshit . . . this plan that you came up with. Ain't no fuckin' turning back now," Eric boomed, waggling his finger in my face. It was no use. We were in too deep now. I flopped back down in the chair and just stared at the floor. I couldn't even think straight.

Ten hours had passed, and we had not gotten a call back from my mother or my father's accountant. I had shot up twice and the drugs had worked to keep my mind off everything that was happening. Eric was on edge. He was barking orders at people and he kept pacing around. Eric kept me so high that I didn't think much about the situation. But he was stressing out about it. I could tell he was worried that everything wouldn't go down as planned. He had made some very powerful people in the streets a promise of a lot of cash for their help with the ransom plot and now he had to deliver or else he knew he would never be able to show his face on the streets again. Things got far worse when one of his cronies brought a small TV to the warehouse. He had contacted Eric and told him that he wanted Eric to see the news. We all huddled around the television. Apparently, the story was out, which didn't do anything for the palpable tension around the warehouse and surely nothing for my nerves. I was biting my already eaten down fingernails as I listened to the reporter's words.

"*The search for Virginia Beach businessman Gavin Rich continues. Police say Rich's wife reportedly has not seen or heard from her husband since he left for work this morning. Police found Rich's longtime administrative assistant, Yvette Everett, dead in Rich's office with one gunshot wound to the head. Police do not speculate that Rich murdered his assistant, but they are not ruling out the possibility. Police tell us it is too early in the investigation to speculate about motive or whether the murder can be tied to Mr. Rich's disappearance. The Rich family has not released a statement at this time. We will continue to follow this story.*"

None of us said anything for a minute. I couldn't believe that they were even entertaining the idea that my father might've murdered Ms. Everett and disappeared. Why wouldn't my mother tell the police that she had gotten a call? Did she want my father to look like he had committed a murder and run away? These were all of the thoughts running through my head when they were interrupted by Eric, of course.

"Your mother ain't so stupid after all, huh, rich girl? She obviously didn't tell the police about our call. . . . That's good. That means we should be getting some money today then, doesn't it?" He asked his rhetorical question like I had an answer for the shit.

I just looked at him blankly and shrugged my shoulders. We walked together back into the room where they were keeping my father. They had untied his legs to allow him to use the bathroom. But they had put the tape back on his wrists. I was happy to see that at least he was able to sit up. They had removed the bag too, just had a blindfold over his eyes. That also made me feel slightly better.

"Your wife has the opportunity to save you. Maybe you can speed this up. Tell us where she has to get the money from for your ransom and we will relay the message to her, Mr. Rich," Eric said when we stepped into the room.

"What is it that you want? What happened to my daughter?" my father asked Eric.

Eric let out a loud maniacal laugh. He stepped closer to my father. "Are you worried about your daughter now, Mr. Rich? Is that the same daughter that you threw out of your house?" Eric said sarcastically.

"How do you know about my daughter? Who are you? What do you want?" my father screamed out. He started fidgeting against the duct tape.

"Calm the fuck down! Don't ask me no more questions! The only thing I want to hear from you is where the fuck the money is!" Eric snapped. He stalked back over to where I was standing.

"Has he been asking for me?" I whispered. I didn't know why it mattered to me so much. I guess I still wanted to know how much my father loved and cared about me after he had tossed me aside.

"He's been asking for everybody including Jesus Christ. Megan, that niggah don't care about you. You better remember how he threw your ass out on your ear and didn't give a fuck whether you had food, clothes, or shelter," Eric reminded me harshly.

He was right. I still couldn't get over what my father had

done. Although he told me that he was worried sick while I was gone, he never told me what he had done to find me. I knew that my father could've afforded a private investigator to find me if he wanted to, but he hadn't even hired one. I was angry all over again. Eric was real good at reminding me of just why we had come up with this plot to kidnap my father. I was back to believing in Eric. He was right. My father only cared about himself.

"Yo, E, w'sup with the payment and shit? It's been twenty-four hours now. We ain't got much longer to be sitting around here. Either they gon' pay or we gon' mirk this niggah and his seed," one of Eric's hoods said.

"Damn, niggah, slow down. Three million ain't no little bit of money to gather up. I'ma call the bitch back in a second. Don't be talkin' no murder shit. I'm the only niggah sending motherfuckers to push up daisies," Eric replied. He definitely couldn't stand anyone questioning or undermining his authority.

"You bastards really think you can strong-arm my family into giving you any money? You're not smart enough to hold someone for ransom and get away with it. You must be dumber than I gave you credit for," my father said angrily.

I immediately wished my father would've just kept his fucking mouth shut. He must've had a fucking death wish.

Just like I suspected, Eric rushed over to him and put his hands around my father's throat. I could hear my father gagging under Eric's grip. I knew how powerful Eric's hands were too.

"Listen, you rich motherfucker. All that fuckin' money you got, you probably stole it by robbing from the poor anyway.

Yeah, Mr. Gavin Rich, I did some research on you. I know how you got Indian immigrants to come to this country and get those loans for gas stations and then you swoop in and steal it right from them. I know all about your shady-ass real estate dealings too. I may be a thug in your eyes, but I'm smarter than you fuckin' think. You think the police SWAT team is going to swoop down in here and save you? You think so? I bet you I get my hands on your fuckin' money and I get to fuck the shit out of your wife and daughter," Eric said cruelly.

I had my hands over my eyes. I hated to see him hurting my father like that. But what Eric was saying surprised me. How did he know so much about my father? My mind was racing with a thousand thoughts.

When Eric released his neck, my father fell to the side, gasping for air. He had hit the floor with a thud that sent a chill through me. Everything was coming apart right before my eyes. I wanted so badly to rush over to my father and help him up. Eric would've had my head if I did. This flip-flop of emotions, one minute angry enough to do this to him, the next minute feeling sorry for him and wanting to save him, was killing me. I suddenly had the strongest urge to shoot up. I needed to escape.

"If you hurt him he won't do us any good. Stop letting your emotions get the best of you," I said calmly.

Eric was clearly surprised at my words and how they flowed. He was so used to me being the one to lose it every time. Little did he know, I just wanted him to get me some more drugs to survive through this shit.

"Yeah, a'ight, whatever. He gon' be dead if your mother

don't follow through like she supposed to," he said, walking away from me.

We placed another call to my mother. Eric didn't listen to me and he was still demanding three million dollars. He just would not listen to reason and it was apparent that this was going to be a huge mistake.

"I . . . I don't have that much money," I heard my mother crying into the phone. I looked at Eric with wide eyes, as if to say "I told you so." I knew she wasn't lying. If anything she would have about a million at her disposal. My father was not going to let her have access to that much money. He also prob- ably never told her where he had his money tied up. But Eric was not backing down.

"I guess you don't want your husband to make it out of this alive then. I guess you also want to see your daughter die," Eric growled. That shit surprised me. Now he had mentioned me, which was definitely not part of our plan. My eyes were as wide as dinner plates.

"My daughter? You have my daughter too? How do I even know my husband is alive? How did you get my daughter? I need to speak to them! Where are they?" my mother asked in a panic. She sounded confused.

Eric pushed the phone in my face. "Talk . . . cry . . . what- ever you gotta do," he whispered harshly.

I could not fucking believe him! I pushed his hand away from me. I was not about to speak to her. He had not talked to me about this. I was mouthing the word "no." I absolutely refused to speak to her.

Eric pushed the phone back toward me and he pulled a pistol from his waistband and placed it up to my head. He left me no other choice. I swallowed hard and opened my mouth right away.

"Mommy!" I cried into the phone.

"Oh, my God! Megan! Are you all right? Where is your father?" my mother screamed into the phone.

It was kind of heart wrenching to hear her so distraught. Eric positioned the gun at my temple and urged me to keep talking.

"Mommy, listen to me! You have to do what they say. You have to pay them," I said with urgency. It was real because I had a gun pointed at my head. I needed her to understand what she had to do. I also needed Eric to believe that I was still on his side. He was losing it.

"Megan! How did this happen? Where are you? What did you do!" she screamed into the phone. All of a sudden shit changed. Just like with everything, she was blaming me. She just couldn't for once keep her finger from pointing at me. My mother's accusatory tone made me angry.

"Just give them what they want! Give them the money or else you will lose us. We will be dead by tomorrow," I said, and then I dropped the phone. I didn't have anything else to say and I didn't care if Eric was pissed. He gave me a look and then he picked up the phone and put the disguiser back on.

"Bitch, if you think this is a joke you will be burying your whole family!" Eric boomed into the phone. "You have one hour to call back and I will tell you a drop-off for the cash. Call the police and everybody dies . . . including you!" he threatened. Then he slammed down the phone. He started pacing again and rubbing his chin. It was clear that Eric had the same ominous feeling that I had about this whole thing.

"Yo, E man . . . you already stayed on the fuckin' phone way too long with that bitch. If she did go to the cops they done traced that fuckin' call a long time ago," one of Eric's goons told him. We had never even considered that. Thinking back to my mother's voice, it did sound kind of fake. But you could never tell with her. Just like most of her body parts, everything about Priscilla Rich was fake.

Eric was quiet. He seemed like he was contemplating what his boy had just told him. Eric started pacing even faster and rubbing his chin even more vigorously. He was clearly thinking, deciding what to do next. Shit wasn't going as smoothly as we had planned. If Eric had stuck to the ransom amount I had told him to ask for, none of this would be happening. Whatever the outcome of this whole thing was, it would be on him.

"A'ight, motherfuckers think I'm a motherfuckin' joke around here. It's all or nothing for me now. If the cops gonna trace calls and come, what do I have to fuckin' lose," Eric grumbled. He stormed out of the room we were in and rushed back into the room where my father was being held.

I looked at his friend strangely. Neither of us knew what Eric would try to do next. But we were both clearly thinking that it couldn't be anything good. We gave each other a telling look and it seemed we moved at the same time. We followed behind Eric right on his heels. Nobody expected what Eric did next.

"Yo, E man, calm down. We just need to sit tight. I wasn't telling you about the trace to get you all fucked up. I just want you to be careful, my niggah," Eric's friend tried to smooth things over.

Eric would hear nothing of it. "Y'all must think I'm a fuckin' joke," he mumbled under his breath. He walked over to my father and snatched the blindfold off my father's eyes. This surprised us all. Most of all it surprised me! Up until then my father didn't know who had snatched him up. If Eric was chancing my father seeing his face, it could only mean one thing to me. . . . He planned on killing him at some point.

"You want to see who took you for ransom? Huh? You want to see who set you up?" Eric said, as he grabbed my father's head and jerked it in my direction.

I just closed my eyes and my knees buckled. My father squinted as his eyes adjusted to the light. Then he whirled his head around looking from face to face until he spotted mine. His eyes immediately took on a worried look. "Megan? Are you all right, baby? Did they hurt you?" he asked with genuine concern on his face. My father thought that they had taken me as well. Little did he know, I was a culprit just like the rest of them. I was frozen, rendered speechless. I couldn't believe what Eric was doing.

"Is she all right? Do she look like she is tied up like you? Do she look like anybody is holding her against her fuckin' will?" Eric asked, his words dripping with venom. He started laughing, that cackling, crazy man laugh he'd been doing lately. "She is the one who set you the fuck up! Damn old man, I had given you more credit than that. Y'all rich people are some dumb motherfuckers, ain't y'all," Eric retorted, smiling wickedly as he saw my father's eyes drop low when he revealed my dirty deeds.

My legs finally gave out and I collapsed. "Daddy," I whispered. It was all I could muster up. I was on my knees as if I were begging my father for mercy, to forgive me. My father looked at me and his eyes were so sad. They were pleading, like he wanted me to say that Eric was lying, that it was all a lie, that I would never do anything like that to him.

"Megan . . . is . . . is . . . that true?" he asked me.

I put my head down and burst out crying. "Daddy, why couldn't you just give me the money? Why did you have to throw me away? You did all of this to me! This is all your fault!" I screamed out. I was flipping it back on him. It was my defense mechanism. One I had learned so long ago as a child. I was so accustomed to always making my parents feel like anything that I did was their fault. I really didn't mean to blame him or my mother, but I didn't know any other way to explain how their own daughter could participate in something so horrendous.

"Yeah, Daddy, why the fuck don't you tell your little wifey to give up the money. I'm asking for three million for your safe return. . . . She is acting like y'all motherfuckers don't have it," Eric said, getting up close to my father's face.

My father flexed his jaw. I could tell he was growing angry. He was probably most angry at me. "Fuck you! You little street punk! I have people that would cut your balls off and feed them back to you. You have to keep me tied up. . . . You have to exploit a young girl and her family for money because you come from nothing. You are probably the product of a whore's pussy," my father spat, and let a wad of spit fly out of his mouth into Eric's face.

Eric jumped back, caught off guard. He used his hand to

wipe the spit from his face. He curled his face into a deep snarl. I shuddered because I knew what was coming next. Eric was very sensitive about his upbringing. My father had crossed the line. I was suddenly propelled into action. I knew I had to try to save my father from Eric's wrath.

"Daddy, no! Please! Just be quiet," I begged. My father kept saying shit about Eric. He was talking about Eric's manhood and telling him he was a joke. I knew how violent Eric could get when he felt emasculated. I raced over and tried to come between Eric and my father. Eric pushed me out of the way, and I went flying to the floor like a lifeless rag doll. His boys just stood watching. They didn't want to get involved.

Eric stormed over to my father and punched him in the face so hard my father crumpled down to the floor. Blood squirted from his nose and some shot on the wall.

"Eric, please!" I screamed, scrambling up off the floor. It was too late. I couldn't make it over to him in time. Eric could not be stopped. He stood over my father like a looming black cloud. Slap! Punch! Crack! Kick! Over and over again he hit and kicked my father.

"Yo, son, you gon' kill the niggah and then we ain't gonna get no fuckin' money!" one of Eric's cronies warned. Even they had had enough of watching the assault.

"Shut the fuck up!" Eric spat. He didn't care anymore. I could see it in his eyes, he had lost it. He took a gun out of his waistband. "Anybody that wants some of this right here can fuckin' get it. You either with me, or against me," Eric barked. His brown face had turned almost purple from all of the blood that had rushed into it. There were veins popping out on his forehead and from his neck. He looked like the Incredible Hulk when he was about to change.

"A'ight, niggah, but I'm out of here," the dude said, holding his hands up in surrender and starting for the door.

Eric ran up to him and put the gun to his head. "No fuckin' body leaves here until I get my fuckin' money. I don't trust none of y'all motherfuckers right now! Everybody seem like they getting the case of the pussies up in here. Get the fuck back over there," Eric barked.

The man followed Eric's orders. The other three men that were with him just kept quiet after that. Eric obviously wielded a lot of fucking power.

My father was moaning on the floor and I couldn't look at him. Eric wasn't finished. My father had dissed him and he was hell-bent on making sure that my father paid for that.

"Now back to you, rich guy. You wanted to spit in my face like I'm trash. I came from a whore's pussy, huh? Yeah, maybe you're right. . . . I'm going to show you how the product of a whore's pussy really acts. I'm going to show you how much of a street thug I am. You would feed my balls to me . . . let me show you how," Eric growled as he lifted up his foot and kicked my father square in his balls.

"Agghh!" my father let out a bloodcurdling scream.

Eric laughed. "Maybe you should have somebody cut your balls off now," he said.

"Eric, please!" I screamed out.

Eric just ignored me. He stood over my father and I thought he would hit him again. It was a mess. Instead, Eric hoisted my father up by his shoulders from the back. His hands were still bound so he was defenseless. Eric placed my father in a chair. He could barely sit, his body was wilting. He probably had broken ribs by now. My father looked delirious. I could see that his face was starting to swell and blood was all over his nose and mouth. Eric hit him again. This time blood squirted out of his mouth.

"Eric, please!" I cried again. But my pleas fell on deaf ears.

Eric pulled out his track phone and began dialing a phone number. He listened for a minute and then he went over to my father again. Eric forcefully lifted my father's downturned head. "Lift ya head up, motherfucker. Niggah, you better start begging that fake-ass plastic surgery queen of a wife of yours. You better tell that bitch to get on the good foot with this loot," Eric said, placing the phone up to my father's ear.

"Priscilla . . ." my father moaned. He could barely speak as blood filled up in his mouth. My father took a deep breath as he fought the pain so he could talk. "Shhh, calm down. I am all right. Megan was the one behind this. Her and her little street piece of shit boyfriend. Don't give them shit, Priscilla. This is my hard-earned money. Call the police!" my father called out before Eric snatched the phone away.

I just closed my eyes and shook my head. What a stupid thing to do.

"That's it, you motherfucker! You better pray your wife is not as stupid as you are!" Eric boomed. Then he hit my father with the butt of his gun.

"Ugghh!" my father shrieked, falling over out of the chair. A huge gash opened up on his head as his skin busted wide open. Eric hit him again with the gun. This time I could swear I heard bone cracking. Eric's cohorts were even closing their eyes. My father lay in a heap, now even more bloody than before, and that's when Eric stomped on him. "Ohhh!" my father wheezed as Eric kicked him in the side again. My father suddenly went still. His head was bleeding profusely. I had had enough. I couldn't stand by and let this happen. I thought Eric had beaten him to death.

Blood, there was so much blood everywhere. It was clouding my vision. And the smell. It was so strong and overwhelming. The smell was one I could never forget.

"Aggghhh!" I screamed as my body moved involuntarily. I didn't even realize I was jumping up and down. The sight in front of me was ghastly and I thought I would go into shock. I had stood by and done nothing and now I was going to pay for it. We were going to pay dearly for it, I should say.

"Megan, shut the fuck up! If you scream again it's over! I put a bullet in his ass and end this whole shit," Eric yelled at me. His face was contorted into a scowl I had never seen him wear before. One of his fists was clenched tightly and his other hand gripped a gun so hard that his knuckles were pale. I knew he meant business, so I tried to obey his demands. I clasped my hands over my mouth, trying to keep the screams in. It didn't work. As I looked down again, trying to muffle a scream proved futile. I was brimming with emotion. This whole shit was out of control now.

"What did you do?" I belted out through wracking sobs. I could feel my face swelling from all of the crying I had been doing. There was blood everywhere—on the floor, on the table, some had even squirted on the wall. It was clear that my father needed medical attention and fast. I stared at the almost lifeless form in front of me. Things had gone terribly wrong.

Eric had gone berserk punching and kicking and hitting. It was supposed to be easy. There wasn't supposed to be any violence involved, just a snatch, grab, and collect. "Oh God, Eric . . . What did you do?" I hollered again.

"I did what we planned to do! Remember whose fuckin' idea this was in the first place. Now shut the fuck up and get on the phone and make them believe us now!" Eric growled cruelly. I knew he was right. This had all been my idea. All for revenge. I never meant for it to turn out like this.

"Start fuckin' movin'! I'm gonna snap the fuckin' pictures of his half-dead ass. Just in case your fucking mother don't believe that this shit is serious," Eric continued in the same cruel, ruthless voice as before. It amazed me how he could just stand in a pool of a helpless person's blood and not even care. Eric was definitely not the man I thought he was. My vision had been clouded. Too clouded.

"I—I . . . can't!" I wailed. My stomach was cramping and my entire body trembled. I couldn't stop staring at my father. *What have I done? What I have I done?* I repeated to myself over and over again in my head. I couldn't help but think that this was all my fault. I had done all of this to myself and to my family. Now here I stood feeling like the worst person alive. Now I wanted to just save him—take him and run far away from Eric and his goons that were surrounding him. I wanted to ask for forgiveness for being such a selfish and spoiled little bitch.

"Help me . . . Me . . . gan." My father had finally come back into consciousness. He whispered my name weakly through his very battered lips. That broke my heart. I was so happy he was still alive, but his words and hearing him rasp out my name sent a pang of hurt throughout my body and a cold chill down my spine. How could I have done something so wretched to my own flesh and blood?

"Shut the fuck up! She can't help you. The only one that can help you is your wife and your fucking accountant!" Eric barked, rushing over to where I was standing. "You think I'm fuckin' playing, right?" Eric hissed, walking over and kicking my father again in the side. It was like he was taking pleasure in the shit now. Like he relished someone else's pain and agony.

"Aggh!" my father screamed out in pain. I was surprised he could still muster any screams. I had not even realized I was daydreaming and hesitating to make the call. "Stop it! You said you wouldn't hurt him!" I screeched. The tears were even more uncontrollable now.

"Bitch, if you don't pick up the phone and dial somebody to get the money I will fuckin' kill him and pin all this shit on you! Or better yet, I might just kill your ass too," Eric barked. His face was so serious.

I knew when he was bluffing and this wasn't one of those moments. My hands were trembling fiercely as I dialed the familiar number. I knew that if I didn't do it, Eric would be committing murder for real. I clutched my cell phone tightly against my ear and prayed that the accountant answered. Eric was standing over me menacingly as he brandished his gun so both of us could see it.

"Hello," I breathed into the phone through the computerized voice disguiser. I swallowed hard when I recognized the familiar voice on the other end of the phone. I felt like I would piss on myself. Eric snatched the phone from me. He could see that I had frozen up like a deer caught in headlights.

"We want three million in cash for his release. We ain't callin' again! If you involve the cops, he dies. No second chances! No more calls either!" Eric screamed into the machine.

My heart sank as I looked into the battered face of my father. I felt a sickening mixture of emotions. One part anger, one part regret, and a large part fear. I wished that my parents had never treated me so badly just because they didn't approve of my lifestyle. We could've worked it out. I wished that I hadn't gotten so mad at them that I wanted revenge. That I would have done almost anything to make them hurt as much as I did at the time. I wished that I wasn't raised to be so greedy and self-centered. But most of all, at that moment, I wished that I could rewind time. I wanted this all to be a bad dream. Too bad it wasn't.

8

My Punishment

"C'mon, we gotta move him. Your mom's called and she got the money up." Eric nudged me out of my sleep. I had finally conked out after a long, losing battle trying to fight my sleep. I lifted up my head and it immediately started pounding. I couldn't believe that my mother had really gotten up that much money.

"Where is she going to meet us?" I asked, rubbing sleep from my eyes.

"Down near Princess Anne Road where there is not too much traffic. We will release him to whoever drops off the money. I'm telling you, Megan, if I even feel the slightest bit like your mother went to the fuckin' cops, I'm popping his ass," Eric threatened.

I was so fed up and sick of his fucking threats. I just rolled my eyes. I wanted this all to be over with. "How is he now?" I asked. Eric had separated me from my father because he said I was too emotional after he beat my father up.

"He is alive. . . . That's all you need to know. You better act like you with me. If I think I have to question your fuckin' loyalty this shit ain't gonna work. Tell me what it is, Megan," Eric snapped at me. He was jumpy and antsy as hell.

"I am always loyal to you, Eric. You took care of me when they tossed me out. I am down with you until the end," I said robotically. The truth was, I was deathly afraid of him now. I saw firsthand just what he had been capable of. I was telling him what he wanted to hear. The truth was if I could get out of his sight I would've run straight to the cops and given us all up.

After my father's beating, of course, Eric gave me some shit to get me high. I had shot up a half a bag of meth before Eric announced that it was time for us to leave for the exchange. My mother had called back. I was high so I was more at ease than I thought I would be. That is, until I saw my father. "Oh God," I moaned when I looked at his battered face and body. He could hardly stand up as they led him outside. My father shuffled his feet like maybe his legs were fractured on top of the broken ribs. Everything on his body was grossly swollen. Finally he succumbed to the pain of his injuries and he fell.

"Get up, old man. You only got a few more minutes with us. We get our money and you get to a hospital," Eric said to him. I was silently praying that my father just kept his mouth shut and didn't get smart. If Eric had hit him again, I'm sure he would've died.

"Megan . . . p-p-please. I need a doctor," my father whispered.

"Daddy, this is almost over. As soon as we get the money, you can go to a doctor," I said in a soft tone. That garnered an evil look from Eric. I didn't much give a fuck at that point.

We all started out of the warehouse and that's when all this shit came to an abrupt end. I can't say that when I heard the shouts I wasn't kind of relieved. I really was glad it was all over.

"Put your fucking hands in the air!" I heard a loud booming voice call out.

I whirled around, but it was too late for me to even scream or react. I was thrown down to the ground with a force that had knocked the wind out of me. I could hear the battering of feet around my head. The police were running in every direction. They were screaming out commands and telling people to put their hands up, drop weapons. It was truly like a scene out of television. There were guns drawn and when I looked up, I saw that they had Eric on the ground as well. He looked helpless and stupid all at the same time. A real strong sense of hatred flitted through me. Hatred for myself was probably stronger than anything I felt.

"Eric Chambers and Megan Rich, you are under arrest for the kidnapping of Gavin Rich and the murder of Yvette Everett," one of the heavily armed police officers said calmly. I knew my punishment for this crime wouldn't be light.

When I was hoisted up off the floor I noticed a big SWAT truck, FBI vehicles, and a ton of other law enforcement vehicles. We were in that fucking warehouse and never knew they were closing in on us. We were so fucking stupid and now we were caught.

"Don't hurt my daughter," I heard my father say as they dragged me into a paddy wagon. He was on a stretcher getting ready to be loaded into a waiting ambulance. I couldn't even say a word to him. I couldn't even continue to look at him. I was too ashamed about what I had done to him. I knew I deserved nothing less than the whole book of the law to be thrown at my ass. I was never going to be the same shamelessly rich girl. All of the things I took for granted had flashed before my young eyes.

"This is all your fault, Megan! You fuckin' bitch! You set me up! I can't go back to prison! I won't go back to prison!" Eric was screaming.

I just shook my head as a female officer pushed the top of my head down and loaded me into the back of the paddy wagon. Eric was screaming like a lunatic, sounding so stupid. One of the cops told him to shut the fuck up and when Eric got smart, the cop hit his ass with his baton. I kind of smiled at that. Anything that would cause Eric Chambers pain, I was all for it. It served him right. If he had just stuck to the original plan none of this shit would've happened.

I learned while preparing for my trial that all of the mistakes Eric and I had made during the botched ransom kidnapping had backfired. First of all, Eric making those fucking calls from a landline so he could use that stupid voice machine allowed the police, who my mother had contacted right away, to trace the calls back to the warehouse. Then, Eric's little goons thought they had taken the video from the only surveillance camera in my father's office, but they hadn't. There was a digital video recorder out back, so when the police investigated Ms. Everett's murder, they were also able to see us all clearly on the video. They had the entire kidnapping on tape, with me standing there doing absolutely nothing about it.

When the jury came back within two hours with a guilty

verdict, I wasn't surprised. Still, it hurt. Then to top it all off, I found out that Eric had struck a deal with the prosecution and pinned the entire incident on me. He had made up some story about me convincing him to kidnap my father so I could get insurance money. Eric got a lighter sentence for his cooperation. Me, the shameless rich girl who would've done anything for a man . . . Well, I got just what I deserved.

Life in prison without the possibility of parole.

So as I sit here in my cell penning this story about one of the most shameless acts in history, I will send this message. Rich does not equal happy.

Puttin' Shame in the Game

Noire

1

Like everybody else, Noble Browne had his shortcomings, but baggin-and-taggin the honeys wasn't one of them. You see, Noble was a fifteen-second man. The kind of cat who could spot a chick, lay it down, and get the bizz over and done with in fifteen seconds or less.

Nah, Noble wasn't no Johnny-quick in the sheets, like you might be thinking. He was a traffic cop. One of them red-light, green-light dudes you see standing in the middle of a busy street. Arms all waving, whistles be blowing. You know, they be holding it down and making sure shit flows righteously and everybody stays in their lane.

Noble had joined the police force straight out of college, and he was one of those super rookies you hear about every once in a while. It had only taken him two short years to slide into a spot on the narcotics squad, and when the lead detective came looking for a volunteer to go undercover, Noble knew he was the right man for the job.

For five years Noble wallowed in the trenches pulling off

crazy covert capers. He'd worked on some of the most dangerous undercover drug stings in Brooklyn, and the streets fit him like a hand in a glove. Noble looked like the streets, he spoke with the tongue of the streets, and he had the mad gorilla swagger of the streets too. In fact, he'd become a master at worming his way into airtight drug cells, gaining a criminal trust, and getting solid with the capos.

As an undercover agent Noble jetted from territory to territory, dipping in on the sly—just long enough to get the goods on kingpins and connects—and then setting up the house of cards so it could get knocked all the way down.

But out of nowhere a string of bad luck had choked Noble's shit up, and his entire career changed. And when the smoke finally cleared, Noble found himself ass-out, forced off the narcotics squad. Dude ended up directing vehicular traffic in the city, which for a dedicated street cop like Noble was just half a step up from donut-eating desk duty.

Now, check it. Being reassigned to traffic enforcement woulda prolly cold-crushed a lesser man's ego. After all, helping blind old ladies cross the street was nowhere near as gully as the rush Noble had enjoyed when he was out there pitting wits against violent criminals in Brooklyn.

But Noble wasn't your ordinary type of guy, and none of that loss-of-status bullshit came close to fuckin' with his self-image. Why should it? No matter how many grimy little shit balls life threw at him, Noble was an on-point nig who manned up and played the hand that was dealt him. In fact, he was an opportunist of sorts. He lived his life with his nose wide open, sniffing out the sweet opportunities that were buried deep in the shittiest of situations.

So, instead of tossin' tan goods to trap boys and checkin' for the stick-up kids in the cut, these days Noble was all about making friends out of everyday New Yorkers who walked the streets of midtown Manhattan.

And with his hard-body thuggish good looks on a six-foot-six-inch, muscled up frame, Noble made a *lot* of friends.

Especially with the women.

Noble admired women. All women. He found something beautiful to behold about each and every one of them, and whenever he laid his sexy gaze on a lady he made damn sure she saw her worth reflected in his eyes.

Noble liked to throw his rap down on the job, but he was also dedicated to his duties, because directing traffic was some serious shit. His area of responsibility was the busy intersection at Fifty-ninth Street and Madison Avenue in midtown Manhattan. It was a bustling commercial spot overflowing with educated chicks who had corporate jobs and ghetto needs.

Noble became a student when he stepped into his grid box. He studied the pedestrians who scurried past him every day, and after just six months of chewing on a whistle he had seen it all.

Dig, a real man could tell a lot about a woman just by the way she walked. Couldn't no chick slang it like a New York City chick could, and watching the babes take on the borough, Noble sure liked what the fuck he saw!

There were all types of honeys walking the streets too. Like the high-heeled, dainty ass-strutters, with legs and breasts galore. Noble had 'em pegged as coffee runners and paper shredders. Straight outta the corporate office pool. These were the cold-sexy speculators who kept their shit tight from head to toe 'cause they never knew when some banked-out CEO was gonna step off on his wife and come running to the office pool for a younger, finer replacement.

And then there were those type A chicks. The corporate ladder climbers. Smart, driven, and determined to elbow their way into a world where dicks and nuts ruled. These women were real easy for Noble to spot. They wore their navy blue skirt suits and ankle-high tube socks folded down over their No nonsense panty hose. With Nikes and Reeboks laced tight on their feet, they dashed down the sidewalks of New York with powerful strides, always early, yet still in a damn rush.

Noble respected these women, he just didn't holler at 'em. There was never a chance to. They moved like men. Like they were dashing off to a big-ball-pissin' contest or something. Shit, even with his college degree from Morehouse, a blue-collar brothah like Noble would have to chase one of them chicks like a cracked-out purse snatcher if he wanted to get his fifteen seconds of rap in.

And then there were those women who were somewhere in the middle. These were the kind Noble liked best. They weren't butter soft, but they weren't man-hard, neither. They were just women. Some pretty, some just a'ight, a few were happy, a couple were sad, but almost all of them—the single ones any-way—had something in common.

They were looking for a good man.

More specifically, they were looking for a man who was holding it down in 3-D: a decent job, a nice big dick, and some damn good dental benefits.

A man like Noble Browne.

2

The streets of Manhattan were live and poppin' in the springtime, but Noble was a Crooklyn boy at heart. Brooklyn was his borough, his home. Noble had come up in East New York, the only son of a pawnshop owner. His mother had been a schoolteacher back in the day, but she'd been killed while working with her sister in Guatemala when Noble was just three. The two women had been out for an early morning jog when they were struck by a hit-and-run driver and left on the side of the road to die.

Noble's father had been a neighborhood fence with a smoove legitimate front, and as a tyke Noble had spent countless hours marveling at the treasures that desperate people hocked in exchange for the cool green cash his father never seemed to run out of.

Bam Browne had been a man about his bizz, and he'd taught his only son the value of money—and its potential for growth—at a very early age. As a result, Noble had developed a jones for precious metals back in the eighties, and he hadn't stopped investing in them yet.

"This is for you," Bam had told seven-year-old Noble one day as he handed the boy a heavy box with a burgundy crushed-velvet top. Ever since he was five Noble had helped inventory and chronicle the shop's merchandise, and he was always fascinated by the guns, jewelry, and other valuable items that people traded for pennies on the dollar each day.

Young Noble's eyes had lit up as whatever was inside the box clanged and jangled beneath the lid. He'd been all smiles when he flipped the top open and found a huge jumble of forks, knives, and spoons that someone had pawned for a fraction of their worth, then failed to come buy back within the allotted time.

Staring into the box full of silverware that had probably belonged to some dope fiend's great-grandmother, Noble listened closely as his father explained that he could either keep the property as a souvenir, or sell it and put the money into his savings account.

"I wanna sell it," Noble had declared the moment his father finished talking. "I wanna sell it, but I don't wanna put the money in my savings account, Daddy."

At first Bam had balked. "I thought I taught you better than that. You got a chance to get your hands on some real money and right off you wanna run out and spend it?"

Noble had shaken his head quickly.

"I don't wanna spend it, Daddy," he had assured Bam. "I wanna invest it."

"Invest it in what?" Bam had asked. And Noble, with his eyes glinting as he stared down into the crushed velvet box that held the keys to his future, said simply, "Gold, Daddy. I wanna buy me some gold."

Over the years Bam had taken great pleasure in passing his son various items of forfeited property and watching what the boy did with them. He was proud of the way Noble studied the pawned goods that were brought into his shop, assessing their value with a young, critical eye. Bam began learning about the financial markets just so he could explain the world's monetary system to young Noble, and it made him grin when, instead of buying a bike or some new sneakers with the money he earned, his son jumped on lucrative investment opportunities, usually in precious metals like silver and gold.

By the time Noble was fifteen he had a gold bar stash that was more valuable than most of the houses in their neighborhood, which to Bam's dismay was going downhill fast. Crack was king on the streets of Brooklyn, and even the police were scared to go head-up against the violent drug gangs that the gutters were breeding everywhere.

Bam no longer trusted the security of the large safe that was installed at his shop, so he recruited two of his homeboys to strap up and accompany him and Noble as they transported the boy's precious metals to a local bank where he opened Noble's very first safety deposit box.

As the years passed Noble had opened up many other boxes at many other banks. He was caked up, and not just in metals that the government couldn't trace, but in corporate stocks and bonds too.

The next move on his chessboard was to find himself a good ruby. A woman who was special enough to bear the Browne seed and carry his name. Bam was sick, and he wasn't getting any better. Noble wanted to give his father a grandchild while he could still enjoy one.

He figured he was ready to settle down and get wifed up. He was planning to whip out a ring and propose to a special somebody on his thirtieth birthday, but the woman he chose was gonna have to be more than fine. She was gonna have to be worthy. A chick who wanted him not for the stash he had amassed, but strictly for his love. So, outta all the chicks he'd stripped and dipped over the years, Noble had finally narrowed it down to three girls in particular.

Zsa Zsa, Kiki, and Malisha. Each of these women had something about them that kept Noble's nose open, but the problem was it was way too hard to choose. All three of the honeys were neck-and-neck in the runnings. Beauty and booty wasn't an issue. These girls had it straight locked on the outside, but figuring out the truth about their insides was gonna take some time and some skill.

Noble felt like the chosen niggah on a game show. It was daytime TV drama up in his camp, and his mission was to solve the puzzle, spin the wheel, or roll the fuckin' dice. There was no way around it. If he wanted to find a quality jewel, he was gonna have to dig deep in the dirt. Noble was gonna have to pull back the curtains on his triangle of honeys. He was gonna have to take a nice long peep behind door number one, door number two, and door number three.

3

"Good morning, Officer Noble . . ." The cute little gap-legged chick giggled a merry tune as her body flowed across Noble's intersection like warm molasses. It was a bright Monday morning and her name was Glorious. She had beautiful brown eyes and gorgeous dark-chocolate skin. She wore a white tank top and a pair of red crotch-choker jeans that accentuated her curvy waist and magnificently shaped ass. She grinned and tossed her long mane of curly hair, then winked and gave Noble a hungry, mischievous look.

"S'up, baby," Noble said, and with his whistle clenched between his teeth, he grinned right back. And grinning was all he did too. He knew this girl well. He had banged her a few times before he settled on the three honeys he was currently seeing, and as fine as this chick was, Noble was glad he had left her ass alone.

Glorious was a freak. In more ways than one. She'd put marks on Noble's body that he would take to his grave. Glorious worked the counter at a designer perfume store right up the street, and she had a body so spectacular that the first time Noble saw her he had blown his whistle, held his hand high in the air, and stopped traffic in both directions just so he could watch her cross the street without slowing her stroll.

Of course he hit her with his smoove shit. Noble always timed his game by the blinking numbers that counted down the "walk" signal mounted on the traffic pole. In the fifteen seconds it had taken for Glorious's pink-painted toe to leave the sidewalk, until she stepped her sweet ball of cocoa-colored curves up on the curb at the other side of the street, Noble had stopped traffic, gotten her name, her digits, and found out which borough she lived in.

Noble had hit her number later that night and laid down his ever-persuasive rap. They'd talked until his cell phone got too hot to hold. Glorious rambled on, telling him all kinds of shit. She was working on a career in the perfume industry, her last boyfriend had gotten deported back to Haiti, and in her opinion most men these days were fake-ass liars, so she'd kept her legs closed for the past six months.

"I'm not pulling off my thong until I find me a real man," Glorious had stated boldly.

"I'm real," Noble told her. "As real as you can get."

"Serious shit," she huffed. "I'm tired of all the fake-ass brothahs who either wanna live off a professional sistah, or put his foot all up in her high and mighty ass! So when it comes to getting some of this good na-na, posers need not apply."

Noble was all for that. He was a straight-up nig, and he appreciated a woman who knew what she wanted and laid down the house rules! Matter of fact, he liked it more when he actually had to work for it, and two nights later him and Glorious were chilling at his brownstone in Brooklyn, sharing some Chinese takeout and a bottle of good wine.

They'd done all the usual first date shit without ever leaving the house. They talked about their families, the jobs, where they saw themselves in five years when they got their lives set.

"You look like you set right now," Glorious had complimented him as she glanced around his crib in appreciation. "You living real large for a street cop."

Noble just nodded. He knew his shit was impressively laid out. He'd paid cash for his brownstone back when they were going for pennies on the dollar, and he'd had the interior remodeled to suit his tastes. There were two gas fireplaces in the joint, loads of imported hardwood that had been etched and distressed by hand, granite, marble, antique collectibles, you name it. One of his exes had been an interior designer, and all Noble's furniture screamed quality and class. He collected expensive sculptures, and had them artfully displayed throughout the house. Nothing Noble had was over the top for a dude whose pockets were as knotty as his, but Glorious was right. Noble's economic status was higher than that of ten cops, but of course he kept that info under his hat.

He thanked Glorious when she complimented him again on his setup, as she smiled over the rim of her long-stemmed crystal flute. The wine had them both nice and loose, and Noble was feeling good as they snuggled up close on his sofa and acted like they were watching a karate movie.

But in reality, Glorious wasn't watching nothing above Noble's waist, and his love muscle was sho'nuff throbbing for her too.

"I don't usually be all up in no strange man's house," Glorious giggled as she pressed her wet lips to his neck and slid her dainty hand up Noble's left thigh.

"We've been talking so much that I don't feel like a stranger," Noble told her, rubbing his thumb across her pouty lower lip. Glorious was a real sweet package. He couldn't keep his eyes off her curly hair, smoky eyes, juicy breasts, and thick, ghetto ass.

"But I wanna get to *know* you," she breathed, rubbing up and down the hard muscle of his thigh. "Really, really know you."

"Oh, you gon' get to know me," Noble promised as her hand snaked toward the hammer that was banging in his crotch. He caught his breath as she cupped his package and squeezed it gently between her fingers.

"Damn your shit is big," she whispered.

"Yeah, baby," Noble moaned. "It sure is. And you about to get every inch of it. As much as you can stand."

Noble pulled her to his chest and kissed her, their tongues tangling as he probed and thrust into the wetness of her mouth. Noble hadn't been with a woman since before he'd left the narcotics division, and it was hard to stop his fingers from scurrying all over her juicy body like ants on an apple slice.

They were both moaning now. Humming into each other's mouths. They were as close as they could get while sitting down, and Noble wanted to push her back on the sofa and climb on top of her, but then suddenly Glorious pulled away and stood up.

Noble panted as he watched her. He wanted some of that. The sight of her rock-hard nipples poking through her thin shirt made his tongue tremble.

"Noble," she'd whispered coyly. "We both grown so I'm just gonna put it out there. I wanna be with you tonight. I really do. But I'm scared."

"Scared of what?" he asked. "You're a woman, and I'm a man. And like you said, we're grown. I wanna get with you real bad, baby. I would never hurt you."

Glorious shook her head. "I'm not scared that you'll hurt me, I'm scared you might . . . well . . . judge me. . . ."

Judge her? It was Noble's turn to shake his head. From what he could see, Glorious was simply fuckin' glorious! Phat and stacked. The girl had the type of body every man wanted.

"Judge you for what?"

She looked down at her feet and blinked hard a few times.

"Well, just so you're aware . . . I know I look good, but everything about me isn't quite perfect. Some men can't handle that."

Noble was confused. Her body was a work of art, and she had his drawers straight rocked up. What could be more perfect than what she was holding? Instead of responding, Noble stood and swept her up in his arms. Walking carefully, he carried her into his bedroom. He flipped off the light switch as he went through the door, and he was just about to lay her down on his five-thousand-dollar king-sized bed when she stopped him.

"Hold up," she said firmly.

Sighing, Glorious wriggled out of his embrace.

They stood by the bed, both of them breathing hard like they were ready to get it on.

"Can you cut the light back on, please? I need you to see all of me. The *real* me."

Noble nodded. His eyes were hungry for her and he did like she asked.

When he was standing in front of her again Glorious locked her gaze on his. She reached up and tugged at her hair, and then suddenly her beautiful curly mane was dangling from her hand.

"My real hair is natural," she explained as Noble stared from the large swatch of silky hair in her hand to the half-inch of afro-puff covering her head. "I'm letting my new growth get a little longer, and then I'm gonna start twisting my locks."

Noble nodded. Black chicks and their damn weaves. When would they learn that most dudes were more interested in the hair on their pussies than what was on their heads?

"Cool," he said, and then added truthfully, "I like the way women look with locks."

Noble's dick was still on throb, and her fake hair wasn't about to stop no show. Reaching for her hand, he took the wig from her and placed it gently on his dresser. Then he pulled Glorious back into his arms and held her tight, pressing her coconut-sized breasts into his chest and drooling at the thought of rolling those thick nipples around on his tongue.

Wordlessly, they grinded their lower bodies in sync, dry fucking like teenagers who wanted to tear off their clothes. Noble's dick was straining to bust outta his drawers, and the heat coming from between Glorious's legs had him imagining just how nice and wet her pussy must be.

His fingers crawled over her toned back, then he slid his palms up her sides and brought them around to squeeze those thick, extra-firm breasts.

"Umm, chill for a second," Glorious whispered, pulling away again.

Noble just stood there as she stretched the neck of her sweater out and peeked down into her bosom area. She fumbled around down in there for a moment, and his eyes got wide as she plucked out first the right flesh-colored false titty, and then the left one.

Noble winced. She was holding those juicy, fabulous titties in her hands! To his horror, those bad boys were cinnamon brown, and had stiff little rubber nipples on them!

"I've lost over a hundred pounds," Glorious explained. She chuckled like she was embarrassed, then gave him an awkward grin. "Breast tissue ain't nothing but fat anyway, so 'the girls' were the first things to go. I have to use these," she said, holding up the two firm pieces of molded gel that Noble had been feeling all on, "because I lost the fat, but not the skin. Sorry"—she shrugged—"but my natural breasts sag a little bit. You said you wanted real? Well, this is what's real."

Noble stared at the deflated area of her chest and tried not to frown. *C'mon, dude,* he chastised himself. *Not every woman is gonna have nice big knockers. Breasts—just like dicks—come in all different shapes and sizes.*

"It's all good," he assured her. This chick was turning out to be full of surprises. But it was cool. After all, Noble had a little surprise of his own to reveal. He was just waiting for the time to be right.

Glorious tossed her fake titties up on the dresser next to her fake hair, and then she stepped up on Noble real close again. This time when she pressed herself against him she felt hard and skinny instead of soft and juicy. Her body had a whole different feeling going on in his groin. Noble had liked the other feeling much better.

Glorious raised her chin and they went back to kissing, but when she tried to touch his dick again, it was Noble who pulled away.

"Yo, Glo," he chuckled gazing down into her gorgeous face. "You ain't got no more surprises for me, do you, baby girl? I mean, those *are* your real teeth in your mouth and your real eyes in your head, ain't they? I mean, you ain't gon' pop one of your eyeballs out and play skelly with it or nothing, are you?"

She bust out laughing and punched his arm.

"Yeah, boy! Stop playing. These is my real eyes." She grabbed Noble's hand and pressed it between her legs and humped him. "This my real pussy too."

The crotch of her pants was hot and wet, and Noble could feel how swollen her pussy lips were as he rubbed his fingers back and forth across her fat clit.

He had gotten the top button on her pants loose and was just about to slide her zipper down when she clenched his wrist and stopped him.

"There's one last thing," she said, looking up at him with those soft, pretty eyes.

Noble sighed and braced himself. What the fuck was it gonna be this time?

To his surprise, she unzipped her pants the rest of the way, then wriggled around sexily as she slid them over her curved hips. Her panties were bright orange and looked stunning against her glorious chocolate tummy and thighs. She had him wanting some sho'nuff Reese's Pieces.

"Take 'em off, baby," Noble panted as he grilled her lower body. He cupped his dick through his pants and gave it a nice strong squeeze. "Go head and take 'em off. . . ."

Glorious took them panties off all right.

And she took her whole ass off right along with them.

"What's that?" Noble hollered as she stood in the middle of the floor holding her thick, round, gangsta booty in both hands.

"It's a butt pad," she said simply. "I told you I lost a lot of weight. The booty got a bit jiggly. I wear a pad to round it out."

Noble bucked inside. This chick had seriously misrepresented. He wasn't mad, and he damn sure still wanted to get him some, but he *was* gonna get her ass back.

"All right then," he said, fumbling with his belt buckle. Since this chick wanted to take fake shit off, they could take some fake shit *off*!

Noble grilled her dead in the eye. He unzipped his pants and pushed the crotch down under his swollen nuts, and then with a ruthless grin, he reached inside his boxers and unstrapped his fake . . . leg!

4

Noble had lost his leg doing what he was born to do. Police work.

The stump of his thigh throbbed angrily as he remembered that shit like it was three minutes ago. And no matter how much he replayed the grisly scene in his mind, the truth was he had gotten ganked. Ambushed. Set up.

Noble was one of the few young cats who was well respected in the police department. He had competed against nine other officers for that prime undercover assignment. But when the contest ultimately came down between Noble and some shiesty-looking street cop looking to earn a rep, Noble had gotten the job.

Operation Green Ice was based outta Brownsville's Van Dyke Projects, one of the most crime-infested areas of Brooklyn. Noble had inched his way in good with a power playa called Big Bump, and for five months he rolled like a slanger and pulled felonious drug capers with some of the major bosses on the grind.

A critical buy was about to kick off, and everything was going according to plan. The task force was right on the verge of taking down two high level shot-callers when Noble's shit got flipped.

"Yo, this niggah foul."

They were standing in the middle of an abandoned auto body shop, and the accusation came outta nowhere. Noble looked up and cursed inside when he saw which capo was bringing it.

It was that niggah Dent. A powerful street broker who worked with a connect out of some projects in East New York. He'd been suspicious of Noble from the gate. And now, with the goods spread out all over the table, the distrust in his hooded eyes was cold and deadly, and aimed straight at Noble Browne.

Dent nudged Bump, the dude who had brought Noble in. Bump stood with an AK-47 slung over his shoulder and another one gripped tight in his fist.

"Yo, I'm telling you, Bump," Dent spit. "Ya boy stinks, man. Like a sewer rat. Somebody betta check him."

Noble had cold grilled that niggah. *This fool wanted to check him?* Wasn't happening! Noble was wired up like a goddamn telephone pole. Nah, that shit wasn't happening!

Playing the role, Noble swelled on Dent. His eyes were colder than a winter breeze as he spit, "You might wanna watch your fuckin' mouth about who you callin' a rat, son. Now, we can take care a this bizz and distribute this cash, or we can start tearing off some heads."

Noble pressed his arm close to his side. He was comforted by the feel of his tool digging into his flesh, and the knowledge that there was a team of SWAT cops listening in and ready to blast niggahs out if shit got shaky.

"Either way," Noble growled at the young connect, who as it turned out, had a damn good nose, "you better watch what you say to me, niggah."

Dent was unfazed. That niggah just sneered. His lips curled down but his eyes stayed flat.

"You talk a good one ak, and you probably as G'd up as you come across—" Suddenly his tone dropped low and his knuckles tightened around his heat. "But believing a mothafucka's words ain't why I'm here today. I survive off wit, instinct, and the feelings in my own fuckin' gut, and all three of them things is telling me you's *A MOTHAFUCKIN' COP!*"

Noble couldn't tell who shot him first, but when that hot lead started flying from all directions it wasn't hard to figure out that he'd been peeped and set up.

Falling back on his training, Noble had pulled his gat and started sparking off rounds too. The sound of gunfire exploding all around him was deafening, and with his cover blown, the SWAT team had moved in with their superior weapons and tactical skills, taking niggahs down hard and fast.

By the time the smoke cleared there were bodies strewn all over the greasy garage floor. Including Noble's. He'd taken five hot slugs, three of them hitting him in his right leg, shattering bone, arteries, and other small blood vessels.

Them niggahs had blasted him good. His leg was shot out. There was way too much damage for even the most skilled surgeon to repair, and three hours after Noble got to the hospital his right leg was amputated five inches below his hip.

Rehabilitation had been a real bitch, but Noble had taken it on the chin, like he took everything else that life dished off. He worked hard on his physical therapy, and always went above and beyond what the trainers told him to do. It took a minute, but he persevered, and the next thing he knew he was being fitted with a prosthetic leg and was back on his feet.

But a one-legged narc was like a pit bull with no teeth, and to Noble's disappointment, a couple of weeks later he received a certified letter ordering him into retirement with full pay and benefits, courtesy of the NYPD.

But Noble wasn't going out like that.

While government benefits and free money was always cool, Noble had no need for that little-ass paycheck they were trying to dish off. At the age of twenty-nine he wasn't nobody's retiree. He was a cop, and he had paid for that title with his flesh and with his blood. Wasn't nobody gonna sit him down like some old dog that needed to be put up on the porch.

Even with one leg Noble was still young and fit, his mind was sharp, and his pockets was crazy swole. So he got bizzy. Noble cashed in a couple of departmental favors that was owed to him, and a few weeks later the medical board reversed its decision and came up with a creative plan for his career path.

On paper, Noble would still be a cop and receive all officer pay and allowances. But on a daily, he would be on loan to the Traffic Enforcement Agency, where he'd pull duty as a traffic officer in midtown Manhattan. No, he wasn't gonna be out there ganking kingpins and bustin' bad guys no more, but he wasn't gonna be at the crib chillin' on the couch neither.

Noble gave it some thought and decided he was cool with it. He would have to give up his gun, but he would get him a whistle. Without further hesitation, he signed the agreement and reported for duty at the TEA.

Noble was back in uniform, and once again life was sweet.

5

"You stupid bitch!" the young chick barked. Eyes blazing, she burst outta the doors of Fine Headz with a plastic smock draped around her shoulders and wrap lotion slicking down her hair.

She snatched the parking ticket that Zsa Zsa had just slid under her wiper blades, then balled it up and threw it in the street.

"I ain't paying that shit!" the girl spit. "The meter just ran out two minutes ago. All these goddamn criminals running around New York and your dumb ass is out here fuckin' with *me!*"

Zsa Zsa Flynt rolled her eyes as the young guttersnipe clanked quarters into the expired parking meter and talked mad smack. Zsa Zsa didn't care whether the chick picked the ticket up outta the gutter or not. If the fine didn't get paid on time, the price was just gonna get higher every day. And once the city added on all those penalties and interest and shit, sistah was gonna wish she had just went on and paid the $115 and been done with it.

The young girl was steady beefing as Zsa Zsa moved on to the next illegally parked car. She straight hated her job. She wasn't built for this shit. The nature of her grind was all about freezing in the winter, getting soaked when it rained, and burning the hell up in the summer.

For two long years Zsa Zsa had been pounding the concrete and choking on smog in midtown Manhattan. And like most NYC meter maids, she had been through it all. She'd been cussed out by all kinds of crazy sickos, had the shit smacked outta her by a rusty old white man, and had got bitten on the ankle by a poodle for writing his owner a double-parking ticket three days in a row.

Zsa Zsa had never wanted to punch no clock or be nobody's employee. Matter fact, due to her creative skills, and the prize package she was holding, she didn't feel she should have to work a regular job at all. With her half-Asian, half-black, hot beauty blend, and a sistah's curvy body that had been turning heads since she was twelve, she felt she should have been draped over some boss's arm and living her dream life. Instead, she was busy walking up and down the street in a monkey suit looking stupid and feeling unglamorous.

Zsa Zsa knew she was special, and not just because she was fine, neither. There were plenty of beautiful sistahs out there, but not many of them had the eye for fashion or the nose for business that Zsa Zsa had.

For as far back as she could remember there had always been a sizzling spark in her that was trying to burst into a flame. Zsa Zsa was into fashion and she wanted to do big things. If given the opportunity, she knew she could launch the next major black clothing line and straight shock the fashion world. Her designs were so cold her line could break out like Nelly's Apple Bottoms, or Beyoncé's House of Deréon, or even Kimora Simmons's urban fiyah line Baby Phat. Zsa Zsa would do *anything* for the chance to live her dream life. All she wanted to do with her life was create amazing fashions that could be sported by everyday women, or styled by chicks who were rich and famous!

But even getting close to her dream was damn near impossible. For one thing, she was broke. And for another, she had a court order that dictated that she get a job and keep it for at least three years. When Zsa Zsa thought about how her life had gotten so turned around she wanted to kick herself up her own dumb ass.

Consumed by greed and open on her own good looks, Zsa Zsa had bellied up to a local drug boss who had a serious gambling jones. Not only did he distribute drugs, they had stayed at the racetrack cheering on his horses. And for a long time his hand was hot and he raked in big bank. But the minute that fool's horse started losing he had turned on Zsa Zsa. He got it in his head that she was some kinda bad luck charm, and one night he locked her in his crib and tried to beat all the mo outta her.

Zsa Zsa was done. Dude was clearly mental, and she wasn't the type to take an ass-whipping and come back for more, but old boy wasn't tryna let her go. She moved out of her cousin's house and went to live with her aunt, but he still followed her. He'd be hiding all up in the bushes and shit, or tapping on the windows at night, scaring the hell outta her auntie.

Zsa Zsa knew some loco shit was gonna go down if that niggah didn't leave her alone, but she had never imagined how bad it would be. One night when she came home he was waiting on her aunt's stoop talking about they needed to talk. He said if she took a little ride with him and let him explain himself, then they could both move on and he would leave her alone. Something had told her not to get in his whip, but he was chill tonight and looking sane in the face . . . damn, was it a mistake!

As soon as she got in he locked the doors and took off driving faster than shit. He was laughing, Zsa Zsa was screaming, and people on the streets were scattering outta his way. That fool didn't care who he mighta hit. Kids, women, old ladies . . . It was like he had a death wish, and he wanted to take Zsa Zsa with him.

It wasn't long before flashing lights were behind them and sirens were wailing in the air. Zsa Zsa thought about jumping out the car, but they were going too fast, and plus he had the doors locked. She knew he was crazy when he snatched her handbag off her lap. He steered the car with his knees and she saw him take something off the seat and stuff it inside her bag. Zsa Zsa figured it out when he rolled down his window and tossed her handbag clean out, but by then it was too late. That fool pulled the car over like everything was cool, and their high-speed chase was over.

But Zsa Zsa's problems were just beginning. The cops had muscled both of them outta the car and smashed them into the concrete at gunpoint. They were taken straight to the precinct, and since his drugs had been found in Zsa Zsa's bag, she'd gotten knocked and carted off to Rikers Island just like any other petty criminal.

But the judge had had a little mercy on Zsa Zsa after her drug test came back clean. He had believed her when she said she was not involved in the drug game, had never personally used drugs, and was definitely not down with selling them.

And it was all true too.

Zsa Zsa had been grateful when the judge offered to drop the charges and seal her record on the condition that she find employment within ninety days. She had taken the competitive exams for a couple of city jobs about a year or so earlier, and as soon as she was released from Rikers her auntie had hooked her up with an interview at One Police Plaza in the offices of the Traffic Enforcement Agency.

She had been relieved to get the job before her ninety days were up and she had to go back and face the judge, but even as she was going through the whole hiring process, Zsa Zsa had known the gig was only gonna be temporary.

For one thing, traffic enforcement agents might work for the police department, but they were *not* cops. And out of all the TEA employees, meter maids were the doo-doo on the bottom of the shoe, the most hated people in uniforms. Besides, did she really wanna be out there walking the damn streets writing tickets all day? *Hell no.* She wasn't tryna wear out the bottoms of her goddamn feet! She was tryna start her own empire, not ruin her life with a thirty-year career.

So day in and day out, Zsa Zsa had been scheming on a way to accomplish her goals. If she was ever gonna have a chance to quit her job and do her own thing, she'd have to catch herself a good man. One who could sit her down and bring her inside out of the cold. A man who had the means and the moolah to set her up lovely, and help a flamboyant mami get her bizz up off the ground so she could rub shoulders with the stars.

Zsa Zsa sighed and glanced at the diamond-specked watch that the guy she was seeing had bought her. Instead of buying her all kinds of pretty *stuff*, what she really wished he would do was get down on his knees and ask her to be his *wife*!

She smirked. Dude was a winner and he had her heart and all that. And he was definitely a card-carrying member of the big dick club. But he had some shit about himself too. Papi knew he had options and choices, and he'd made it clear that he was seeing other chicks. He said he was gonna let them all know who he'd chosen on his thirtieth birthday. Well, Zsa Zsa wasn't really the man-sharing type, but she had some birthday plans for him. Whoever he was banging, they couldn't have been wiping it on him the way she was. Convincing Noble that she was the right woman for him was just gonna take some time and some skills, and Zsa Zsa was steady working on her plan.

She sighed again and wiggled her aching toes around in her ugly work shoes. She was dying to dip into the Chinese restaurant across the street and get off her feet for a little while, but she had an appointment to catch that she'd been dreading all week.

There was a whole fleet of meter maids walking the streets of New York City, and a few of her ditzy blond-haired coworkers were some sho'nuff sistah haters. Them white girls been dropping big dimes on Zsa Zsa for ducking into pizza parlors during work hours, or for getting her shop on when she was supposed to be out there burning the skin off the bottom of her feet and writing parking tickets.

For the third time in six months, a supervisor had run up on her chilling with her feet up in a sandwich shop, and Zsa Zsa had sworn up and down that she only went inside a restaurant or store if she had to use the bathroom. The supervisor was a young Puerto Rican guy, and he had been more interested in Zsa Zsa's tits than the words that were coming outta her mouth, and she'd been able to wiggle her way outta that infraction.

But just recently one of them jealous coworker bitches had managed to mess her up again. Juicy Couture was having a crazy sale, and Zsa Zsa had dropped a fat scoop of cream on fashion wear that fit her toned body to a tee. She was rushing outta the store carrying sick shopping bags when she ran right up on two white female supervisors.

She was busted! One of them white hoes had set her up! Since it was her third malingering infraction, Zsa Zsa had been ordered to report across town to see the boss man. Of course she was nervous and pressed about it, but she was hoping to just get written up and maybe docked a little bit of pay, and perhaps it wouldn't go no further than that.

She glanced at her watch again, then looked around at the cars parked at the meters and wondered if she was being watched. Yeah, envious eyes were probably crawling all over her, just waiting for her to mess up so they could stab her in the back and try to get her fired. She hated white chicks!

On the real, she did have time to write at least four or five more tickets before she needed to catch the crosstown bus to see the chief, but bump that. Zsa Zsa had a check that was about to burn a hole in the bottom of her designer purse, and she needed to get to the bank.

Clipping her ticket pad to her waist, Zsa Zsa eyed a black Nissan that was double parked at the corner. The driver couldn't have been worried about being seen chillin' in a no-parking zone because ridiculously loud music was blaring from his windows. She moved a little bit closer.

A ruff-looking dude with a red doo-rag on his head sat behind the wheel with a cigarette dangling from his lips. Zsa Zsa glanced around to see if any other meter maids or maybe even a street cop was anywhere nearby. When she saw none, she smirked, then rolled her eyes, then turned around and started walking in the opposite direction. All that "enforce the law at all costs" shit was a bunch of bull. She wasn't about to roll up on no hood niggah in midtown and get the shit slapped outta her.

Instead, she eyed a dirty white Taurus whose meter was real close to expiring. She had ticketed this car many times before, and couldn't believe the owner was too dumb to come outside and feed the damn meter. *Well, whoever owns this nasty-ass whooptie, they about to get another damn ticket!* The meter still had close to ten minutes on it, but Zsa Zsa wasn't about to wait around for somebody who was in the habit of letting their flag go up. The driver of this car was a serial illegal parker, and whoever it was, they didn't deserve no sympathy. She whipped out her pad and got to writing.

The bank was only a few blocks away from where her boo worked directing traffic, and after sticking the ticket on the gritty windshield, Zsa Zsa fell in with the crowd of frenzied walkers as she broke out to cash her check.

Like everybody else on the streets of New York, Zsa Zsa kept to herself. She walked like she was about the bizz, her hips rolling hard with her stride. And even though she was dressed in a monkey suit/play-cop uniform, her flowing hair and bomb body still attracted mad attention.

She walked up to Fifty-ninth Street and peeped her man standing in his grid square with his arms waving and his white gloves gesturing. Even from the back he was fine. Tall, built, nice muscled-up ass . . . you couldn't even tell he was missing a leg.

Her boo had been shot in the line of duty and had most of his right leg amputated. And although it had been kinda awkward in the bedroom at first, Zsa Zsa had forgotten all about that stump the moment she felt his snake sliding all up in her.

In fact, she had been so impressed with his sex game and so proud of him for having the balls to get his leg shot off and still get back up on his feet, that after she rode his dick until it faded into the sunset, Zsa Zsa had stood up on the bed and proclaimed Noble Browne her wounded warrior, and then she reached down and gave him a butt-naked high five!

With a slight smile on her lips, she pushed through the doors of Omega Bank and scanned the crowd. "Damn," she cursed under her breath as her smile flipped over to a frown. The line was long as hell. It snaked around the lanes twice, and the waiting customers stood talking on cell phones, texting, or just gazing around impatiently.

Zsa Zsa got behind the last person on line and prepared to

wait her turn. She had been coming to this bank for a while and there was always a crowd. Every few minutes she shuffled forward a few steps as the tellers finished with one customer and called for the next person in line. It took a good ten minutes before she was close to the front. And when she finally did get up there she glanced at the next available teller and rolled her eyes.

How come I had to get this stuck-up bitch? Zsa Zsa thought as she reluctantly walked over to the station of the one teller in the whole bank that she couldn't stand.

The name tag outside the teller's window read *Malisha Chambers,* and the chick sitting behind the thick bulletproof glass had a distracted look on her face.

Zsa Zsa took the check from her purse and pushed it through the slot.

"I need to cash this, please."

She hated coming to this girl's window. For one thing the chick worked slow. It seemed like she counted out every dollar at least fifteen damn times. And she was a pain in the ass too. Zsa Zsa had been cashing checks there for two whole years, but every time she stepped up to this teller's window the chick acted like she had never seen her before.

One time Zsa Zsa had forgotten her ID card at home, and even though the girl had just cashed a check for her a few days earlier, she had nutted up and played dumb. Zsa Zsa had fumed while the chick took a year to go to the file and look up her signature, and still after all that, she had held the check all up in the air and studied it like it might be fake.

"It's a damned government check!" Zsa Zsa had damn near shouted, but the girl had paid her no mind. She made Zsa Zsa sign the check in front of her, twice, and then told her she needed to go to the customer service desk and get an approval.

Zsa Zsa wasn't up for no shit outta Ms. Malisha today, and she was pretty shocked when the girl didn't give her none.

"You have to sign it," the teller said, looking away as she pushed the check back through the slot.

Zsa Zsa nodded and picked up the pen that was dangling from a wire bolted to the counter. "I know. I was waiting to sign it in front of you."

Bougie bitch! She signed her name and pushed the check back through the slot.

"Wait a minute!" Zsa Zsa said quickly. She dug in her shirt breast pocket. "Here's my ID."

The girl looked up briefly.

"I know who you are," she said softly, then put her head back down as she worked on the check.

Zsa Zsa was shocked. Not just because the chick was acting all mild mannered and was about to cash her check without seeing her ID, but the girl just didn't look right. She looked wiped out. Her hair was usually butter, and her makeup was always on point. Zsa Zsa had figured her for one of them uptown bitches who thought she was cute. Or maybe she was a flosser from somewhere up in Harlem.

Wherever the heffah came from, she *was* real cute, Zsa Zsa had to admit, and her style was usually classy and airtight. But today she looked whipped in the face. Tired. Shot out. Like life had jumped on her back and was dragging her through a Canal Street gutter.

Zsa Zsa didn't have a drop of sympathy for her ass though. Why should she? This chick worked indoors and sat on her ass all day! Her damn feet were probably feeling just fine! Without giving the teller another glance, Zsa Zsa scooped her money up and stuck it in her purse, then jetted out the bank so she could get across town for her mandatory misconduct meeting.

She was speed walking as she headed toward the bus stop. As much as she hated her job, she couldn't afford to get fired, and after everything they had on her, being late to see the boss just wouldn't look good for her.

"Hi, Noble," she called as she crossed the intersection of Madison Avenue and stood at the bus stop. He waved, and a grin spread across Zsa Zsa's face when she noted the look of stunned appreciation in his eyes.

Standing near the bus stop, Zsa Zsa leaned against a light pole and posed for her man. She knew she was a banga. Her entire package stood out from the crowd. With her jet black, slightly curled hair that always looked windswept, to her flawless light brown skin and slanted eyes, she didn't need nobody to tell her she was beautiful. Her round ass and tiny waist were just an added bonus, and the bouncy breasts that stood out prominently on her chest were like a cherry at the top of a creamy, delicious milkshake.

"Hey, baby," Noble said, removing the whistle from his mouth so he could flash her his gorgeous white smile. "I thought you were working down below Fifty-fifth Street today. What you doing up on this end?"

"I'm about to catch the bus across town. I need to take care of some business," she said vaguely, acting all nonchalant. Zsa Zsa knew how to keep a niggah guessing. Keep him on his toes. Most men just wanted to fuck her. She had accepted that as a fact by the time she was twelve. But for the few who actually wanted to get in her head, and for the one or two she truly gave a damn about, she had learned to keep the mystique going. The less she revealed about herself, the more they wanted to know.

Zsa Zsa had first met Noble right at this very intersection, and within seconds he'd coaxed her cell phone number right outta her mouth. She'd been surprised when he called her just a few hours later, and she'd listened carefully as he told her a little bit about his life.

Of course, she'd been impressed. A fine-ass dude like him, with no kids or baby's mamas, and who had a job and a crib *and* a car? For a moment Zsa Zsa had felt stupid to even be thinking about hooking up with a guy who probably only made about forty grand a year. Her crazy-ass drug kingpin had spent more than that on her during a weekend in the Cayman Islands. Shit, he'd tossed away more than that at a single horse race.

But after her short stint on Rikers, Noble and his little city job would definitely do. Zsa Zsa was done with the drug lords, the gamblers, and the ballers. She didn't want no dude whose résumé consisted of multiple upstate bids, or a string of street pharmaceutical gigs in three different boroughs. Those types of guys were just short-term solutions to her long-term needs.

Nah, Zsa Zsa was looking to latch on to somebody legit. Noble had told her he was looking for a wife, and she was damn sure hunting for a husband. She longed for a steady square with a regular paycheck, and maybe some decent health insurance too. A guy who could fuck, and wasn't gonna start swinging on her whenever his horse got an attitude and ran too slow. Somebody who was mentally stable and wasn't gonna be jumping outta no bushes tryna get at her. A dude who might not be ballin' and droppin' a gwap of money on the races every night, but who would support her in becoming a business owner, and provide her with some real security in these tough economic times.

A dude like Noble Browne.

6

I'm gonna have to start stripping again, Kiki thought as she envisioned the solid grand she used to rack up in titty bars every night. She eased up off the gas and guided her bus toward the curb, then put the gears in park and released the door lever.

The hydraulics hissed as a gorgeous black girl with straight hair and Asian eyes got on the bus and swiped her Metro card. Dressed in the blue getup of New York City's uniformed force, and displaying the name *Zsa Zsa Flynt* on the tag, the girl was so pretty that Kiki smiled at her without thinking. She reminded Kiki of a mixed girl she'd gotten down with in a ménage à trois for a rich guy back in her college days, but of course it wasn't her. This girl was thicker and way cuter, but the cut-throat look she shot Kiki was full of unmistakable hostility.

"Screw you too," Kiki muttered as the gorgeous girl rolled her eyes and swung her curvy hips toward the back of the bus.

With her hand on the door switch, Kiki waited while a fat old man struggled to climb the three steps as a group of teenagers rushed to get on behind him.

After closing the doors, Kiki glanced into her side-view mirror, then rotated the heavy steering wheel and swung the city bus out into the crowded lanes of midtown traffic.

There was a time not too long ago when she wouldn't have been caught dead riding a city bus, let alone driving one. But things had really changed in her life, and these days, instead of shaking her boobs and stepping out of her silk panties for top dollars, the blond-haired, blue-eyed Kiki Lyons earned her living making the wheels on her bus go around and around.

Kiki had been a good little white girl from the burbs of Long Island growing up. But during her freshman year at Seton Hall University she was introduced to quick money and horny men, and soon after she'd started stripping for the thrill of it.

Sweet-natured and gorgeous, Kiki had been a natural on the stage. She had no problem catering to the dark fantasies as she rode the golden poles and touched herself in public three nights a week. She actually got high off the power she felt radiating from her pussy. It made her feel desirable and in control. And the money was damn good too. In fact, Kiki could have stripped for years and stacked mad cream if she hadn't caught a serious case of jungle fever.

Like a lot of college dorms, hers was no better than a Forty-second Street ho house. With her long blond hair and an extraordinarily bouncing ass for a white girl, Kiki was known as the white girl with the black body, and she had all the slick brothers in the dorm on rock. She ended up getting with the school's star running back, but then got left on the sidelines when he dissed her for a Puerto Rican chica with a brighter smile and an even bigger ass.

But there were plenty more black athletes where that one had come from, and Kiki wasn't by herself for very long. By the end of the semester she had fallen in love with another football stud, and this one hung around just long enough to get her pregnant.

She gave birth to her son in the middle of her sophomore year, and she dropped out of school a year and a half later after she delivered her daughter. As a single mom with two kids, Kiki found it tough to make ends meet, so when her father took sick and invited her to move into his small house and help share the bills, she packed up her kids and jumped on it.

Driving a city bus wasn't Kiki's idea of a high-tech career, but it was the only thing she had going on. Sure, she could get another job in a strip club in a hot minute. And she could pull it off too. Her body was still tight and fine after having two kids, and there were no sagging titties or stretch marks to mess up her smooth white skin. Hell, feeding her kids franks and beans three times a week made a few hours of topless dancing look like a great career choice.

Stripping was a seedy, underbelly job. All those hungry eyes on her body, the countless grasping fingers pinching and groping her all night. Men seemed to worship her body, and Kiki actually got turned on from all the attention.

But there were a few things holding her in check. For one thing, she lived with her sick father and it would kill him if he found out his darling daughter was creaming in her underwear for strange black dudes every night. And for another thing, Kiki had two kids to think about. As much as she loved being naked and adored, she never wanted to do anything to degrade herself in their eyes, or to set a bad example for her daughter.

So, with nowhere else to turn, Kiki hauled her tail outta bed every morning, microwaved a bowl of oatmeal for her father, rushed her kids off to day care, and then plopped her ass down in the driver's seat of the M3 bus like a good little girl.

And even though she stayed broke, Kiki was very grateful to have a job at all. She got paid on time, had a good retirement plan, and belonged to a city union. But with the responsibility of raising a family resting entirely on her shoulders, her little paycheck just wasn't enough. The money Kiki brought in the door went flying right back out the window for bills, groceries, and child care.

The recent problems with her health just added more drama and uncertainty to her life. And it had Kiki scared like a mutha, too. She just didn't understand it. Out of nowhere she had started nodding off. Going straight to sleep. She could be sitting down reading, or brushing her daughter's hair. It didn't matter. One second she would be minding her business and doing what she did, and the next thing she knew she was opening her eyes. She never even remembered falling asleep. Only waking up.

At first it had been easy to just brush it off. Kiki knew she was tired and overworked, so she started putting the kids down earlier every night and getting in the bed to cop a few more Zs, but it didn't help. No matter how long she slept, she'd nod off anyway.

She had already caused two accidents on the job, and they'd given her a warning and put her on written notice. Kiki couldn't understand how she had crashed that big old bus, especially twice, but one minute she was sitting at a traffic light with her foot on the brake, and the next minute her bus had gone through an intersection and crunched up a parked car.

Kiki had thanked God that nobody had been hurt either time, but she'd had to lie to her supervisors to cover her ass. The first accident she blamed on a slippery patch of ice on the street, and after the second one she swore up and down that something had gone wrong with her brakes.

Kiki had served a thirty-day suspension and been required to go through an intensive driver's safety course before she could be restored to driving duty and full pay. Those thirty days of no pay had damn near sent her and her kids to the poorhouse. With no savings and only her father's small disability check coming in, Kiki had been tempted to crawl back on a stage and throw her thong on the floor, but instead she had dragged her kids into food pantries and soup kitchens until her pay came through again.

Kiki's supervisors really liked her a lot, and they sympathized over the situation with her father and her kids. But they'd also warned her that if she had one more driving accident—whether they liked her or not—her ass was out the door.

The thought of not being able to provide for her kids was terrifying. In desperation, Kiki had gone to see a local doctor who was not affiliated with her job's insurance plan. She paid him all this money outta pocket just for him to tell her he suspected she was suffering from a disorder called narcolepsy. He urged her to visit her regular physician, who could then order a thorough sleep study and give her a firm diagnosis.

But Kiki wasn't about to do nothing like that. City bus drivers were required to stay awake on the job. People's lives were in their hands, and the public trust was at stake. If Kiki rolled up on her supervisor talking some shit about narco-any-damn-thing, she might as well just pack it up and take it to the crib. Her job would be a wrap, and so would her only source of income.

Kiki was despondent. Life wasn't supposed to be this damn hard. Especially for a cute white girl like her. Wasn't no need in looking to her babies' daddy for help because his ass had five other kids that he wasn't taking care of either. The last time Kiki called his mother's house asking for help, she had gotten straight cursed out.

"Did *I* get you pregnant?" his drunken mama had demanded. "Did *I* climb on top of you and hump them babies up inside you? *I* didn't lay down with nary white girl and get me none of her nasty pussy, so all y'all pink-slit tricks betta quit blowing up my damn phone looking for money!"

That had been the last time Kiki had dialed the only number she had for him, and she had promised herself that she would never get low enough to call her children's grandmother again.

Sure, there had been other dudes who she probably coulda gotten with if she put herself out there. Black dudes were suckers for white girls with ass and hips, even ugly ones. But the type of guys that hollered at Kiki were just leeches. They were all looking for a dumb white girl to reach in her purse and upgrade their status. And Kiki wasn't about that. She couldn't even take care of herself and her kids, so she wasn't thinking about taking care of no man.

Besides, not every dude was good enough to be bringing around her kids. She didn't need no slouch. Life had already made a slouch out of her. She needed a man who could help her pay some bills.

All of this had been weighing heavy on her mind as she pulled up at the corner of Fifty-ninth Street one sad day. The intersection was a change point in her route, and Kiki was required to wait for another bus to arrive, and then she and the driver were supposed to switch routes.

The first time Kiki noticed the traffic cop waving his arms in the intersection she couldn't take her eyes off him. He was real tall, muscled up, and had pretty brown skin. A few days later, Kiki's transfer bus was running late, and she had gotten off her bus to wait. She had been leaning up against a light pole lost in her thoughts, and it scared the shit outta her when the traffic dude blew his whistle real loud.

Kiki's eyes had opened wide and her mouth fell open too. The traffic guy was looking dead at her. He had stopped cars in both directions, and was motioning with his white-gloved hands for her to cross the street.

"No, no," she had stammered, shaking her head and waving her hands. "I'm not crossing!" she had yelled over the noise of the city. "I'm waiting for my bus! For my *bus!*"

To Kiki's surprise the guy had come over to her and struck up a conversation, and almost immediately, Kiki's imagination had taken off big time. She could actually see the setup. The possibility was there. Dude was a traffic cop. He had a secure, steady job and could hold it down for her while she got her health issues under control.

Six months later, her and the traffic cop, whose name turned out to be Noble Browne, were still talking. In fact, they were doing a lot more than talking. At first it had been just nightly phone calls and winks and waves during the day as she transferred buses at his intersection, but it had quickly progressed to something more.

Kiki really liked Noble, and she wasn't tryna come across as no jump-off, so she let him chase her for a good minute before she gave up the booty. But when it finally happened, she had been shocked out of her mind! Noble was fine and had a rock-hard body and a nice, heavy package and everything, but he also had a stump where his right leg should have been.

She had absolutely not seen that one coming, and immediately, Kiki's heart had gone out to him. She'd felt so bad for what he'd endured that she had wanted to plant comforting kisses all over his body.

But Noble's missing leg didn't stop him from handling his love thang in the sheets. He was good for a nice, strong dick down, and by the time they were done fucking like bunnies their first night together, Kiki was practically in love with everything about the dude.

It wasn't just that Kiki had a thing for black men, even though she did, but this one-legged black man was a good-ass catch. He had told her he was looking for a wife to marry, and the fact that he'd warned her he was seeing other women didn't even mess with Kiki's head. She already knew she was the one. Noble had been sent to save her. She just needed him to hurry up and realize it before she lost her job and her kids starved.

Over the past few months Kiki had been dreaming about how straight her shit could be if only she had a good man to help her out. On the real, her father was so sick he wasn't gonna live much longer. And when he died, his little check was gonna die right with him. On top of that, Kiki knew her days were numbered with the transit authority. It was only a matter of time before she fucked around and nodded off again behind the wheel, and as much as they liked her, Kiki knew they would fire her ass on the spot.

She also knew she should probably give up her license and stop driving altogether. The last thing she wanted to do was run over some innocent pedestrian with that big-ass bus. But what was she supposed to do? She had kids to feed and a father to take care of. She had to put food on the table and keep the damn lights on.

It seemed like the weight of the whole world was leaning on Kiki, and she didn't know how much longer she could handle it. If shit didn't change in a hurry, she was definitely gonna have to go back to stripping.

What Kiki needed was a man to help her out. Somebody to step up to the plate and take charge. A man who could hold it down for her and her kids until she could get her shit together and her medical condition straightened out.

What Kiki needed was a savior. A man who wasn't tryna find the fantasy dumb blond chick, and who wasn't scared to get with somebody who already had kids. A man who was capable of shouldering some of her responsibilities so she could catch her breath and rest for a minute.

A man like Noble Browne.

7

Malisha Chambers didn't know a damn thing about baseball until the doctor pulled her into his office and told her that her man was about to die real young.

For months nobody could figure out what the hell was wrong with her husband, Jamel. He had been shaking and bumping into walls and falling down left and right, but nobody could ever tell Malisha why.

"It's called Lou Gehrig's disease," a specialist finally told her. "Jamel has a disease that's named after a famous baseball player. There's no cure for it, and it's gonna kill him fast."

But like the old folks always said, doctors weren't God and they didn't know every damn thing. And as it turned out, baseball wasn't what took Jamel out after all.

Malisha did.

It had been raining, and she'd been rushing Jamel and their young son home from a birthday party when she ran a red light and wrapped her BMW around a telephone pole. Jamel had been killed instantly. Their son, Trey, had been critically injured, and Malisha?

Oh, Malisha had walked away without a scratch.

In a matter of moments every single dream Malisha had shared with her man had been shattered. The cute little house they'd bought in Queens, the white picket fence, the brand new luxury whip . . . none of that shit meant a damn thing without Jamel by her side.

All Malisha had ever wanted was a family, and her husband had been everything she could have asked for in a man. Jamel had been a dependable provider, a dedicated father, and a delicious lover. But when she buried him on that cloudy morning in June, she had put her life right in that hole along with him. Everybody kept telling her that Jamel probably would have died from his disease soon anyway, but Malisha knew it was her act of stupidity, not no damn baseball disease, that had sent her husband to an early grave.

So it was their boy Trey who Malisha lived for now. Her smart, active baby had suffered brain damage in the crash, and was now just a whisper of the kid he should have been. Trey had been discharged from a rehabilitative facility a year earlier, and he required around the clock care. Malisha wanted to stay home and take care of all his needs, but unfortunately, she had to work and earn a living to support the two of them.

The home health aids that were paid for by the city had been trifling as hell, and Malisha had to stay on them to make sure they did the simplest shit right, like cleaning his breathing tube and changing his position in the bed every few hours.

Trey's doctors had urged Malisha to put the boy into a long-term care facility, but she couldn't bring herself to do it. She didn't give a damn what they said about Trey's brain damage being too severe for him to know who she was. Her son knew her! And despite the accident being her fault, he loved her too. Why the doctors couldn't see this, Malisha didn't know. All she knew was that when she looked into her boy's eyes she saw all the love he had for her shining back at her.

It was true that Trey didn't talk, play, or dress himself like other kids his age did, but one thing her baby did was smile. That boy *smiled*! Malisha lived for that smile. And the only thing that was guaranteed to penetrate the fog in her son's brain and put a big smile on his face was music. Classical music. But not just listening to it. Playing it.

So, three days a week Malisha and Trey made the drive uptown to a very expensive school of music therapy, where trained instructors propped him up on a stool and guided his small, stiff hands through endless renditions of classical piano pieces.

At first Malisha couldn't believe her baby was actually pressing the keys and playing the notes, but the smile on his face and the beautiful melody coming from the piano was enough to make a believer out of her.

Malisha was convinced that she had found the key that could permanently unlock the gates of Trey's mind, but unfortunately, the state only paid for a limited number of therapeutic lessons each year. When Trey's benefits ran out, the boy retreated back into his shell, and Malisha could see his smile— and the light in his eyes—dimming more and more each day.

So like any good mother, Malisha had made a decision. If she couldn't get the state to pay for Trey's lessons, she would scrape the money together any way she could. It didn't matter if she had to rob, beg, borrow, or steal, her son was gonna get outta that bed and get his three music lessons every week, come hell or high water.

In the beginning, Malisha had felt ashamed each time she dipped into her cash box at work. She'd been working at Omega Bank since way before the accident, and the people she worked with had been damn good to her over the years. She convinced herself that she wasn't stealing from the employers she respected and cared about. All she was doing was pinching off the profits of a large corporation full of greedy shareholders and a corrupt board of directors.

Hell, Malisha rationalized as she slid a hundred-dollar bill from the stack of money she had just counted down and slipped it under her skirt. Tellers didn't get paid no kinda real wages anyway. They were responsible for hundreds of thousands of the bank's dollars every day, yet most only made about ten bucks an hour for their duties.

Malisha had never been one to come up with a light drawer. Almost all the other tellers came up short every now and then, but Malisha was careful. She double- and triple-counted every penny she gave out, and she never gave out a dime more than she was supposed to.

So, the first time her tally sheet failed to equal out, she was met with astonishment from her supervisors, but not a hint of suspicion. After all, Malisha was human, just like everybody else. It was easy to miss a crisp new hundred-dollar bill when you were counting out thousands all day. Those new bills stuck together like crazy, and it wasn't unusual for even a seasoned teller to be short at the end of the day.

Malisha knew she had to be careful about when and how

she took money, because Trey's lessons had to be paid for in advance. She cut corners and tried to make ends meet from her paycheck as much as possible. She stopped eating lunch with her coworkers, and took leftovers from home instead. Personal grooming and appearance was very high on Malisha's list of priorities. It was something the bank really stressed too, but Malisha gave up her bimonthly trips to the hairdresser and the Korean nail salon. She permed her own hair, and pried off her acrylic tips and polished her own nails when they chipped.

But no matter how carefully Malisha tried to balance what she had and what she needed, she just wasn't a thief at heart, and when she slipped up, she slipped up big time.

The bank had recently conducted an annual internal audit, and some sharp-ass white girl had smelled a big fat rat while examining Malisha's old tally sheets.

Why is it that this teller started coming up short so regularly six months ago? Her shortages have totaled exactly five hundred dollars every month. Is there something going on in her life? Why hasn't this been annotated on the branch's monthly infraction report?

Malisha knew she was in hot water when the branch manager called her into his office. He was a portly middle-aged white man who had always been nice to her. But as Malisha sat down across from his desk, she could tell right off that he was not about the bullshit.

"We'll make this quick, Malisha," he said, peering at a printed report on his desk. "You've been coming up short. Regularly. And in a way that makes it obvious that you're not making simple mistakes in your counting." He took off his glasses and leaned back in his chair. "What you're doing is, you're stealing."

Malisha's mouth had shot open and a string of protests and denials fell out. Hot shame crept up her neck and she was actually fuckin' offended that this fat bastard was sitting there calling her a liar and a thief!

"Save it," he said, deading all that indignation tumbling from her lips. "I've been in this business long enough to recognize a case of sticky fingers when I see one. So tell me," he continued calmly, "which one of your bills are you having trouble paying? Whatever it is, it's costing you about five hundred dollars a month. So what gives?"

Malisha sniffed back tears of guilt and shame as she opened up to the bank manager and begged him for mercy. She thanked him for being so understanding after the accident, and for all the books and stuffed animals he'd bought for Trey over the years. She told him how big Trey's smile was when he played classical music on the piano. She told him how desperate she was to keep that smile on her baby's face.

"Honestly, Mr. Wortman," Malisha pleaded. "I've been working here a long time. You know me. I'm not a thief," she sniffed. "I'm trying to be a good mother. Trey wouldn't be in his situation if it wasn't for the mistakes I made that night. I'm sorry I stole from y'all. I just didn't have anywhere else to turn."

"Well, turning to your cash drawer is certainly not an option," he said. And then his eyes got softer as a kindly look crossed his face.

"Look, Malisha. You are a good worker. One of our top employees. And I like you. I really do. It was a tragedy, what happened to your family, and everybody here feels bad about it. We really do. But let's face it. We're running a business here, and you've broken the law. There's no way the bank can foot your son's tuition at his music school. I don't think I have to tell you this, but you can't just go in your cash drawer and take whatever you need, no matter what you need it for. Like I said, every employee at this branch feels awful about your situation, but your personal expenses are *your* personal responsibility."

Malisha could only nod wordlessly as he spoke, because she knew the white man was speaking the truth.

"So here's the deal," Mr. Wortman said, his voice growing cold and businesslike again. "You've got two choices. Either you pay the bank a restitution of all the money you've stolen, or you get fired. If I have to fire you, then you'll never get an employment recommendation from us, and there's a possibility that you could be prosecuted. The only thing I can offer you is a little extra time to repay the bank, Malisha. But that's it. *You have got to pay.*"

Malisha spent the next few weeks in a state of constant worry. After making the first two restitution payments to the bank there was barely enough money left in her account to buy Trey's food, let alone pay for his music lessons.

But Trey had to have those lessons! As his mother, this was the least Malisha could do for him. She had to give her son a reason to smile. She just had to. The sight of him laying in bed limp and listless was enough to make her want to put a bullet in her head.

If you could gather up all the guilt in the universe, it wouldn't have come close to what Malisha was feeling as she left work for the day. The dude she was dating had offered to bring dinner over for her and Trey, and even though she had played it off like she had to think about it, deep inside she was grateful they wouldn't have to finish off the can of Spaghettios she had leftover from the night before.

Malisha thought about the man she was allowing to get deeper and deeper into her and Trey's life. This guy named Noble Browne. They'd developed a real tight relationship over the past few months. Noble had said he wanted to find him a wife, and even though he'd admitted from the gate that he was seeing other women, Malisha was trying damn hard to make him forget those other bitches and concentrate his attention strictly on her.

See, Noble was just the type of guy she needed right about now. He was honest and he was dependable. He put it on her in the sheets, and he was loving and gentle with her son. True, he had a fake leg that kinda freaked her out, but Malisha tried hard to ignore the sight of it when he was on top of her and it was propped up against the damn bed. The first time she'd seen it, she'd almost screamed. He shouldn't have snuck it on her like that! They had been kissing and touching and all that, and when Malisha had run her hand innocently down his thigh it had felt like she was touching a tree. And the stump. Oh, that stumpy part that was left of his leg. Malisha couldn't even look too close at that. It straight messed her up.

The good thing was, you couldn't even tell Noble was an amputee unless he took off his pants. He walked and did everything else just fine. He had told her about how he had convinced them to let him stay on the force when they had wanted to retire him. He was still a cop, just assigned to work traffic control, and he got a big plus in her book for that.

But there *was* something else that had Malisha wide open on him too.

Noble was gwapped up. *Paid.* Richer than a mothafucka!

Luckily, he was the type of dude who didn't mind spending money on her and Trey. Whenever Noble was around, he paid for everything. Malisha had never once had to dig in her purse in his presence. And even though they had to lug around Trey's wheelchair everywhere they went, Noble liked taking them out. To dinner, to the movies, to the park. Wherever.

The problem was, Noble gave her *things,* and not cash *money,* which is what Malisha needed to pay her bills. It wasn't like he was stingy with his doe, it was more like he was careful. He'd buy her jewelry and gifts, and he had even used his credit card to get her air conditioner fixed, but he had never offered to pay her car note or her rent.

Of course, Noble had no idea what kind of financial trouble Malisha was in, and she damn sure wasn't about to tell him. He wasn't gonna be able to guess neither, because Malisha kept herself up. It wasn't like she walked around looking like she was two steps away from a soup kitchen. She looked like a stunna, and she played that role like a champ. Her clothing was quality, and she always looked classy and sexy. Even if she was dead broke.

Malisha knew Noble was standing on a pot of gold because she'd met him when he came into the bank to fill out an application for a safety deposit box.

As luck would have it, the girl who usually handled the job

had just been promoted, and when the branch manager had asked Malisha to take Noble downstairs to the vault, she'd jumped right on it.

Noble had handed in his application, then chose one of the biggest damn boxes the bank had to offer.

"What you gonna put in there?" Malisha couldn't stop herself from blurting out when the tall dude dressed in a police uniform had pointed at a box that looked more like a safe. "Your car?"

Noble had laughed, and the sight of his ultrabright smile and warm brown eyes made something stir in Malisha.

"Nah, I'm not gonna drive the 'Vette up in there," he said chuckling. "You ain't gotta worry about that."

But a few weeks later, Noble was back in the bank and he asked for Malisha specifically by name.

"Hi," she'd said after closing her teller's window and meeting him at the customer service desk. It wasn't every day that a customer had a teller paged for service, but her supervisor was grinning and shucking like Noble was somebody important instead of a regular old traffic cop.

"Anybody at the desk could've helped you in the vault," Malisha told him, even though she was flattered that he had specifically requested her. "All you need to do is sign in on the log, and we'll get you the control key."

Noble had grinned.

"I didn't want just anybody. I wanted you."

Malisha looked up into his strong, rugged face. That thing she'd felt the first time he smiled up at her was there again. But stronger this time. A whole lot stronger.

"What you want with me, Mr. Browne?"

"I want your number," he said boldly. Then added, "And I wanna show you something too."

Malisha had almost shit when they used their keys to open the box, and Noble stepped back to show her what was inside.

"What in the world is that?" she asked, stunned. Her mind just wouldn't let her believe what her eyes were seeing right in front of her.

"It's gold," Noble whispered softly. He stared at it with mad respect, and Malisha almost felt like they were in church. "Gold bars. I collect them."

Close ya damn mouth! Malisha chastised herself for acting like she'd never seen money before. Of course she had. Tens of thousands of dollars passed through her hands every day, and at any given moment there was more than a million dollars sitting right inside their vault. She wasn't pressed out at the sight of mega dollars. But mega gold was something else. She'd never really seen it in bar form before, and she damn sure didn't know any men who were stacking it like this dude was.

She forced her eyes off the glittering metal.

"You're a traffic officer, right?"

Noble nodded, then smiled.

"I'm wearing the uniform and carrying the badge, ain't I?"

Malisha shrugged. "Yeah, you are. But I didn't think traffic cops made that kind of money in New York. I must be working the wrong job."

This time Noble shrugged. "Or maybe you're just working it the wrong way. I've been investing in gold for a long, long time. If you hold on to anything of value long enough, your bottom line will go up."

Malisha smirked. "Not in this crazy economy. I started buying bank stock four years ago when my son was born, and what I got back then for thirty-five dollars a share, is going for five dollars a share today."

"Yep," Noble agreed. "I know it looks bad right now, but that's the flow of the economic cycle. I invest in stocks and bonds too. And if you hold on to them long enough they'll eventually do better."

"Yeah, okay." Malisha was doubtful. The value of her little bit of stocks had damn near dried up. If she coulda got something decent for cashing them in, she woulda cashed those babies in a long time ago. "If you say so."

"I tell you what," Noble had offered. "How about I take you out to dinner and we can talk more about the market? I can give you a few tips about investing in gold that might make you a much better profit than what you're getting on other commodities right now."

Malisha shook her head.

"Nah, that's okay. I'm straight."

Nobled pressed her gently. "You said you have a son, right?"

"Yeah." She nodded. "I do."

"What's his name?"

"Trey."

"And he's four? I love little kids. How about the three of us hang out together sometime and grab a bite to eat?"

Malisha sighed. She loved eating out. She remembered the days when her and Jamel used to hit plenty of nice restaurants. Jamel would always put Trey next to him in a high chair and feed his son right out of his plate. Those days, like most of Malisha's other good days, were gone forever.

"Nah," Malisha said, shaking her head. "For real. That's okay. My son was disabled in an accident. He uses a wheelchair and it's kinda hard for us to get around in my tiny car. I can usually only take him out a few times a week, and that's for his music lessons. Other than that, we're pretty much homebound."

"That's not a problem," Noble said, then added smoothly, "I like kids and I like music too. I also have a nice-sized SUV. I can help you take Trey to his music lessons, if you let me. What do you say?"

With just a moment's hesitation, Malisha said yes.

It was lunchtime, and Malisha was crossing the street to get to her car when out of nowhere a city bus ran the red light and started rolling through the intersection.

"Watch it!" she screamed, jumping back just in time. She glared at the driver, who she could have sworn had just had her eyes closed. She was a white chick with long blond hair, and she stomped on the brakes right after Malisha screamed.

"You need to obey the damn law!" Malisha yelled as the white girl mouthed, "I'm sorry!" and the bus moved on. Malisha was pissed. She knew all too well what could happen when stupid people made driving mistakes. "I'm the one who had the damn light!" she screamed as the bus continued down the street.

She watched the bus pull over to a crowded stop at the corner, and she was tempted to run over there and curse the white girl out for damn near clipping her, but Malisha's anger turned into sorrow as she crossed the street and caught a glimpse of her white Ford Taurus.

"Oh, hell no. I know I don't see what I think I see," she whispered under her breath as she jetted farther down the block. She had timed herself, and there was no way her meter should have already expired. *Please no, please no, please no . . .* but when she got close enough to see what was up, she bust out in tears.

Another parking ticket was waving from her grimy windshield.

Why me? Malisha screamed inside. She rushed over to the meter and saw that there was still two minutes left on it. How could she have gotten a ticket when the meter was still running? How the hell was she supposed to pay the twenty or so tickets she already had when she could barely afford to put quarters in the meter every day?

Malisha started stressing. She had already gotten a ton of notices about her unpaid parking tickets. She was about to be considered a scofflaw, and pretty soon these city fools were gonna put a damn boot on her tire. And how was she supposed to get to work for two weeks out of the month then?

After paying her restitution to the bank and putting a little bit down on all her other bills, she only had enough money left over for a week's worth of Metro rides each payday. That meant, every other week she was broke and ass out. The only reason she was able to get to work on those off weeks at all was because Jamel's friend Poppy worked at a gas station and he hooked her up with a few extra gallons on her nonpay weeks.

Malisha climbed in her car and put her head down on the steering wheel. She was ready to fall out from stress and exhaustion. She hadn't been sleeping at night because every time she closed her eyes her mind either took her toward the horror of reliving the accident, her money problems, or the shame of getting caught stealing from her job.

If she had just gone home the usual way! If only she wasn't in such a damn rush! In all that rain, why in the hell had she been driving so fast anyway?

Part of her wanted to get mad at Jamel for leaving her and Trey alone with no life insurance, but she forced herself to squash that noise in her head. *It's your damn fault you have to raise Trey alone!* Malisha chastised herself. *Jamel wanted to be here! You had a damned good man!*

And it was true too. Jamel might not have been able to leave them a phat insurance policy or nothing, but at least he had taken care of them while he was alive. Her husband had been a do-right man. The kind of black king who rode a big white horse and made sure his queen and his castle were protected every single day.

And Malisha really missed that. She missed having a man to hold her close and slay life's dragons for her. She needed her a warrior. A battle buddy. A combat soldier who would just bust up in the joint and blast all her troubles away. Malisha need a man who could help her stop reliving the past and show her the way to a future. A man who could be a father to her son. She needed another do-right man who would get up and check on Trey in the middle of the night. Someone who would drive her baby to his music lessons and pay for them too.

A man like Noble Browne.

8

It was the last day of a long workweek when Noble looked up and saw a familiar face from his past. Friday afternoons were always the jump-off for his weekend. He had no problem putting in city work for five days straight, but his weekends were all about mentoring high-risk little boys and showing them how to become a good black man, or chilling with one of his honeys and showing her how she was supposed to be treated by a good black man.

Noble had a full weekend ahead of him, and he wasn't gonna be neglecting nobody. Tonight it was gonna be all about sexy Kiki, and since tomorrow was Saturday, he'd promised to take Zsa baby to a merchandise fair down in the garment district, and later on in the day he was planning to take little Trey uptown to his Saturday music lessons, and then chill with Malisha for the rest of the night.

Standing in the middle of his grid, Noble mentally reviewed his game plan. His body was waving traffic through and nodding at pedestrians, but his mind was definitely on his three chicks. Noble was imagining the freaky lap dance he was sure to get from Kiki, when he spotted her: Sissy Tarver.

Fine ass, sweet-titty, gangsta booty, Sissy Tarver.

Sissy was a number one stunna. Tall, and lumped up in the front and in the back, she had caramel skin, hazel eyes, and long, thick hair.

The last time Noble had seen her he'd just lost his leg. Sissy had been working at the hospital and had recognized his name on a medical chart. Noble had been too doped up and out of it to really talk to her then, but looking at her now brought his adolescent years flooding back to his mind.

Noble and Sissy had gone to Thomas Jefferson High School together, which was located deep in the heart of Brooklyn. Back then, the student body had consisted mostly of rowdy kids from Brownsville and East New York, and over the years the rate of crime, dropouts, drug use, and assaults had soared sky high.

Noble had been one of those kids who managed to straddle the fence and ride the line in high school. He'd rolled hard with his manz and got down with multiple honeys, but he also got his work done in class and studied hard to get into college.

Back in those days Noble had been tall and good looking, but on the skinny side. He wasn't a basketball star, or a standout on the football team or nothing hot like that, but he was chill and well-liked and smoove with his flow game. Popular with the girls, Noble had snuck his hands into his fair share of cookie jars. But the one chick that he'd really wanted—the chick that *every* swinging dick nig in the entire school wanted— had been way outta his reach.

And now, the sight of Sissy Tarver making her way across

Noble's intersection brought back all of those old horny-young-dog memories. Sissy had been the typical around-the-way girl. She'd lived next door to Noble's favorite aunt in the projects of Brownsville, and as a young girl she had come up fast and loose.

Raised by her alky father, Sissy had a rep for giving it up hot and dirty. Dozens of nigs claimed to have gotten some of that, and dozens more were on a waiting list trying to get some.

Noble had been one of them dudes always waiting on the list.

Sissy was crazy-fine back then, and she had a way of moving her grown woman's body that made the rest of the girls at Jeff look like preschoolers. Just like all the other young dicks, Noble had been bent on her. He'd spent hours fantasizing about banging her up against a locker, on the school staircase, or up under his fuckin' bed, if he could.

The juicy sex Sissy was rumored to lay down on a niggah was exactly the kind of freaky shit that Noble's sixteen-year-old hormones were raging for. But between the star athletes and the corner thugs, Sissy's shit had stayed locked up. A regular dude like Noble couldn't even get close to her, because Sissy was a choice piece of ass, and only ballers with high status or mad doe to spend were invited to step up in her grill.

It was during their senior year that Sissy had fallen off. First her father had died, and her uncle moved in to take over the apartment, and then Sissy upped and dropped outta school with only six months left to go. Word on the ave was that she was pregnant by a local drug dealer, and not too much after that Sissy got knocked by the blue boys and sent upstate for transporting drug money for her baby's daddy.

But Sissy's life troubles didn't cast no shade on Noble's game. He'd graduated from Jeff, and gone on to college and forgotten all about Sissy. At Morehouse there had been plenty of chicks with banging bodies just like hers, and Noble had slapped bellies with as many of them as he could.

It was sometime later when Noble's aunt told him that Sissy had served a two-year stint in prison before her lawyer got her out on some kind of technicality. But even though Sissy had come home to the projects and started getting her shit together, the daughter she'd had while in prison had already been placed in the foster system and was lost to her.

And now, watching Sissy Tarver move toward him stoked up some real old feelings in Noble's gut. She still looked good, and she still moved her body the same way, but after more than ten years her lumped up parts were more like puffed up now. She was in no way fat, but she wasn't high-school tight, neither. All that long curly hair that used to catch Noble's eye was gone too. She had a shoulder-length cut that was a'ight, but it didn't even come close to looking as sleek and glamorous as Noble remembered it.

"Noble Browne!" Sissy yelled, waving as soon as she peeped him.

Noble stepped out of the grid and met her on the corner.

"S'up, Sissy," he said, leaning over to give her a friendly kiss on the cheek. "Good to see you again."

"Nah," she grinned, flashing that cute dimple that used to drive boys like Noble wild. "It's good to see *you*. So you're up on your feet and back at work, huh? It was crazy hearing that you'd got shot. I came by your hospital room one day but you were asleep. The next time I came back, you were gone. Discharged to a rehab facility, somebody said."

She held her arms out and looked Noble up and down appreciatively. "It looks like whatever therapy they did for you in there really worked."

Noble grinned and nodded. "Yeah, the rehab was pretty tough, but I made it through. I'm just glad to have a job and be back in the swing of things."

Sissy nodded. "Oh, I knew you'd be up and at it in record time. You were one of those real determined dudes when we were growing up, Noble. Always pushing and striving. I wish I had been more like you back then."

"Hey, it's all about finding a way to pull ourselves up when we get down," Noble said, then smiled real bright. "And it looks like you did that for yourself, Sissy. You still wearing scrubs, so that means you're still working at the hospital, huh?"

She nodded. "Yep. I passed my boards, and now I'm officially a nurse. I just landed a job at the hospital up the street, and it's good to be working and filling in wherever I'm needed."

It was Noble's turn to nod. "Cool. That's what's up. You seen my aunt Cathy lately?"

"I see her every day," Sissy said. "She's been real sick over the past few months, so I try to get over there early in the morning, and then I usually call her at night to check on her."

"You still living in the apartment next door to her?"

"Yep. I sure am. With my uncle. You should swing through and see her sometime. She's always talking about you. I know it would mean a lot to her."

"I'ma do that," Noble said firmly. His aunt had been one

of his biggest cheerleaders when he was a kid. She was a constant in his life, and even though she was sick and couldn't get around too tough anymore, when he got shot she'd sent his favorite homemade sweet potato pie to the hospital to cheer him up.

"Yeah," he repeated. "I'ma do that."

Noble was shamed to learn that Sissy had been spending time and taking care of bizz with his fam, yet he hadn't even remembered to drop his Aunt Cathy a phone call.

A car horn beeped and Noble glanced toward his intersection, and then kissed Sissy's cheek again and told her goodbye. The sight of her had just thrown a curve ball in his weekend plans, and a couple of his honeys might have to get bounced around a little bit on the schedule.

"I'ma swing by this weekend," he called over his shoulder and assured Sissy as he headed toward his grid box. He watched her hips sway down the block. "Yeah. I'ma definitely do that."

9

Noble's first stop on Saturday mornings was always the barbershop. His father Bam had started taking him to Baldy's when he was three, and after staying up half the night putting in work with Kiki, Noble got up bright and early and spun his fresh Mercedes 550 GL down the streets of Brooklyn.

He thought about his sweet little white girl as he sat in Baldy's chair. Their sex thang had been scrumdeelicious, and he couldn't imagine where the innocent, soft-spoken honey had learned to move her body like that.

"Damn," he'd said as Kiki stood in front of him on one leg and raised the other one almost straight up in the air. After using her lips and tongue to roll a condom down over his dick, she had stood up to model her crotchless thong and fishnet stockings. Noble could only moan as her toned legs scissored sexily, and the soft blond hairs on her pussy peeked out from between her split thighs.

"You real flexible, baby," he said admiringly as she threw

her head back and curved her spine in a backward C. Her lus-
cious hair was so thick and long it actually touched the floor
behind her.

Grinning, Kiki had wound her spine in a counterclockwise
direction as she slowly lowered her leg and raised her upper
body. Standing straight up again, she danced to some imaginary beat that seemed to be banging through her soul. Her
eyes fluttered closed as she gripped her milkshake-thick titties
and played with her strawberry-colored nipples.

"Let Papa handle that for you," Noble panted as he reached
out and encircled her taut waist with his big hands. He guided
Kiki closer as she wriggled and gyrated and got both of them
all worked up.

Noble pressed his lips to her breast and sucked her erect
pink nipple onto his tongue. Kiki moaned and squeezed her
thighs together as a jet of hot cream leaked from her pussy.
Still licking and sucking, Noble cupped her soft mound and
tangled his dark fingers in her silky pubic hair. He rubbed her
juicy clit for a moment, then he slid his thick middle finger
up inside her wet pussy and bit down on her nipple.

"Oh, yeah," Kiki moaned. Her hips rocked deliciously as
Noble thrust his long finger in and out of her with a steady,
erotic rhythm. Her pussy leaked pure sugar, and pretty soon
the palm of his pumping hand was full of her sweet cum.

Removing his finger from her slurping wetness, Noble
pulled Kiki closer, then held her by the waist and lifted her
straight up in the air. Kiki was extra cooperative as she held
her legs out and then straddled his lap. Noble positioned her
pussy over the head of his rock-hard dick, and Kiki gasped as

he entered her and filled her slit with eight inches of throbbing black dick.

Using his strong arms, Noble raised and lowered Kiki over his lap. The muscles in his arms and chest flexed and rippled as he controlled the rhythm, pace, and speed of her ride. Kiki held on to his shoulders and enjoyed the thrill. She felt a little off balance due to his missing right leg and thigh, but she compensated by pressing her big toe to the floor and using it for support.

With her pussy getting thoroughly soaked and scuffed, Kiki leaned back so Noble's dick could pound her from a different angle. She looked down between their bodies and saw all that big black wood going up in her gut, and just the contrast between their skin was enough to make her lose it. She pressed his face to her breast and guided her aching nipple into his mouth, and then she came hard. Bucking like a bull. Hard enough to rock them on the chair. But Noble had her. He held her tight as her body shook and shuddered with pleasure.

And he kept right on holding her as she leaned forward and slipped her tongue between his lips. Noble was almost there too. He slid his hands under her jiggling ass and pumped up into her with greedy, demanding strokes. His dick felt so hard and swollen he was scared he was gonna bust out of the condom. Instead, he bucked crazily three more times, then exploded like a bomb and filled the thin piece of plastic to the brim.

It was a damn good thing Baldy had a smock over him because just thinking about how good he'd fucked Kiki had Noble's dick rock hard and aching in his pants. The girl was a beast with her body, and Noble could see himself wanting to stay up in those guts for a good, long time.

But there were other chicks who were demanding of his time as well.

It was like Zsa Zsa had a lo-jack on him or something. Noble's dick had gone down, and he had just gotten up out of Baldy's chair and laid a twenty on the old man when his cell phone rang with Zsa Zsa's special ringtone.

"If a bitch get a attitude, pop it like it's hot!"

Noble snatched the phone off his waist.

"Hello?"

"So since Baldy's finished, are you ready to come to get me?"

Damn! This chick was on it!

"How'd you know he just got done? You sitting outside with some binoculars on me or something?" Noble couldn't help it. He looked over both his shoulders, then ran over and peered out the front plate-glass window.

"Where are you?"

Zsa Zsa laughed. "I'm at my crib. Where do you think?"

"I don't know," Noble said half seriously. "For all I know you camped out on a rooftop somewhere with a tracking device on my ass."

"Noble Browne!" Zsa Zsa laughed again. "You play too much!"

"Who said I was playing?"

"You better be. Are you on your way, or what?"

Noble lifted his chin at Baldy as he pushed through the door and headed to his car.

"Yeah, baby. I'm coming. I gotta run back to the crib and shower real quick, then I'll be on my way."

"Noble!" she whined in her sweet, sexy voice. "That's gonna take too long! Why don't I just meet you at your place? I can clean up while you shower, then we can leave from there."

Whoooa, hell no! Noble almost shouted. Zsa Zsa was a spontaneous free spirit and that's what he dug about her. But the girl was trying to do too much, and lately she'd been exhibiting some real questionable traits. It was bad enough that they both worked for traffic control and she knew a lot of his boys, but Zsa Zsa was nosy as hell too. She was always asking all kinds of questions, and sometimes she tried to clock his moves like she was the chosen one and they were already married.

The last time she'd spent the night with him Noble had busted her going through his contact list on his iPhone. He could have sworn she was using the share contacts feature and sending herself some treasured information. He had started playing her real close after that, and the next time he took her to the crib he'd peeped her trying to clock for the code on his security system!

As much as he was feeling her, Noble had almost dropped Zsa Zsa's ass. He couldn't be with no chick he couldn't trust. And one of his favorite sculptures had turned up missing around that time too. Noble couldn't swear it was Zsa who took it 'cause he'd recently run his other two babes through the bat cave too, but Zsa had been the only one who was overly interested in the sculpture, and she had asked him all kinds of questions about it.

"You got a lot of nice stuff in here, Noble," she'd complimented him, holding up his prized granite sculpture of a roaring black panther. "Why is this one your favorite?"

"I don't know." Noble had shrugged and told her, "Maybe because when I was little I always wanted to go on a safari. I used to imagine myself climbing trees and slaying prey and shit like a black panther. I asked my pops one time if he could take me on an African safari, and he said yeah. I shoulda known he was just bullshitting. I didn't have no mother, so Pops had to work every day. We didn't have time for no foolishness like that. But I've always had a thing for panthers. Safaris too."

Noble had shut the conversation down after that, letting Zsa Zsa know with his body language that he was through talking about it.

"That's really sad," she'd said, ignoring his posture and his silence. "I bet if your mother had been alive you woulda been able to go on your safari. Or at least she woulda figured out a way to bring the safari to you. I'm sorry you never got that, Noble."

Noble knew how much Zsa Zsa cared about him. But she was a lot to handle, though. Once or twice he had been tempted to push her away and leave her alone, but something had always held him back. And it wasn't her gorgeous face or her pretty hair, or those phatty pockets in the back of her jeans neither.

Zsa baby was a head turner, but it was her heart that kept Noble on a string. The girl was straight New York City. A smart, beautiful, down-to-earth Brooklyn girl who could chill with dignitaries at the White House or scrap in a street fight right next to her man. The sculpture that had gone missing wasn't an expensive one or nothing like that, but it was nice, and it *had* meant a lot to him. But then again, so did Zsa Zsa.

It was Fashion Week, and Noble and Zsa Zsa walked into the trade show holding hands. Zsa was excited, and Noble had gotten lifted just off her hype.

He had picked her up in his weekend car, a sweet candy-apple red drop-top Corvette, and Noble had to laugh at the way his girl rode. Zsa was straight bubbly. She had insisted on riding the whole way with the top down and her hair blowing in the breeze as she waved to New Yorkers on the street. And after one look at her stunning face and wide smile, people walking on the streets had no choice but to wave right back at her.

The trade show was being held at the ultra-slick Fashion 26 Hotel, deep in the heart of the garment district. Noble and Zsa stopped at the reception desk to purchase a one-day pass.

"Good morning, sir!"

A chipper white girl with false eyelashes and big blue eyes greeted Noble like she was happy to see him.

"Good morning," Noble said, reaching for his wallet. "We're here for the trade show."

"Certainly, sir. Will that be a ticket for one?"

The white chick had his grill on lock as she grinned up in his face.

Zsa Zsa bucked. "Don't you see more than one person standing here?"

"Oh!" The girl laughed and shrugged. "Actually, my eyes were only on him. Did you want to buy yourself a ticket too?"

The girl was bold, Noble had to give it to her. It was real

obvious she was sending some "free pussy" vibes his way, right in the presence of his woman. Noble felt Zsa Zsa tighten up beside him, and almost laughed. This little snow bunny didn't know who she was dissing. Zsa baby was a girly-girl, but she was also hood.

"Do I wanna buy myself a ticket? Do I wanna buy myself a *ticket*? Is my damn hair blond?" Zsa Zsa demanded, shaking her head. "Check it out, boo boo. There's some shit a chocolate sistah knows that a blond tramp like you will never figure out. If I was the type to buy my own ticket, I'd be the one stuck behind that desk, and you'd be standing here flossin' on this fine niggah's arm! So get your minimum-wage-drawing ass up outta his throat, and give us our tickets before I snatch you by the wig and mop up the floor in this flea-bag hotel!"

The girl looked shook and stunned. Like she was afraid Zsa Zsa was gonna come over the desk and get a piece of her ass. Without a word, Noble passed the girl a fifty and her hand shook as she gave him two tickets. As they turned to walk away, she muttered, "I'm gonna tell my manager you threatened me. And maybe even call the police."

Zsa Zsa was about to blast the girl again, but Noble checked her this time.

"Just so you know," he said, leaning over and speaking softly to the chick, "My lady has good reason to be angry, and you asked for what you got. You were disrespectful to her for no good reason at all, and I hope you learn something from this. All that work you tried to put on me just now was straight wasted anyway. Men like me don't pick up trash."

"See there?" Zsa Zsa huffed as they walked away. "I told

you how they are, Noble. That's why I can't stand no damn white girls!"

Noble put his arm around Zsa Zsa, but he couldn't bring himself to agree. He thought about the hot sex Kiki had put on him just a few hours ago, and how much he always enjoyed spending time with her and her kids. Yeah, he knew some white chicks were straight slimy when it came to the brothahs, but Kiki wasn't loose like that. She was modest and full of self-respect, and carried herself like a lady at all times. Nah, he couldn't agree with Zsa baby on this one, because there were *some* white girls that he liked just fine.

The trade show was packed out, and if there was one special thing he really admired about Zsa Zsa, it was her go get 'em attitude. The girl kept her spirits aimed straight up and full speed ahead. Most sistahs would have allowed the encounter with the sleazy white chick to ruin their mood, but not Zsa Zsa. Her vibe was sky high as she led him from booth to booth while she chatted with designers and examined dozens of colorful sketches.

"This is *me*, Noble!" she shrieked as she raised her arms in the middle of the crowded showroom and soaked everything in. "This right here is sooo *me!*"

Noble grinned.

"I know it is, baby. You graduated from Fashion Industry, right? I don't know what's stopping you from getting with a manufacturer and starting your own fashion line."

She frowned. "Money, honey. Time and money. I wanna run my own business so damned *bad*, Noble. I know I can do

181

it too. I've got the fashion sense and the creative eye to design for the modern woman. People are always asking me where I buy my clothes, and they can hardly believe it when I tell them I sketch and sew all my stuff myself. If I didn't have to grind a nine-to-five every day I'd have time to really let my creative side loose and put my own stuff on the market for Fashion Week. But"—she sighed and gave Noble a puppy dog look—"when a girl has to pay her own bills, then a girl has to work a damn job."

Noble nodded. He pulled her close and kissed her forehead.

"I hear you, baby. But check this out. I'ma have to cut our time a little bit short today, okay?"

"Why?" Zsa Zsa pouted. "You promised to spend the day with me!"

Noble nodded, admiring her smooth skin and the exotic slant of her eyes. He didn't like disappointing her, but Zsa was even finer when she got mad.

"I know I did, and I'm sorry. But something came up, and I've got a little dude I need to check out for a minute."

"Oh, is it one of the little boys you mentor?"

Noble thought for a second before answering.

He didn't make a habit of lying to any of his women. They knew full well that their relationships weren't exclusive, and he was always having to remind Zsa Zsa of that. But still . . . he wasn't about to tell her that he was leaving her to rush over to Malisha's house to make sure lil' Trey got to his music lesson.

"Yeah. I need to spend some time with a little boy," Noble said, keeping it simple. Out of all his chicks, Zsa baby was the sharpest. She could pick up a loose thread and roll herself a whole ball of yarn. Noble knew the less he told her, the less explaining he would have to do.

"But I'm gonna make it up to you," he said, his voice dropping low as he pulled her into his arms.

"How?" she asked, a slick smile teasing her lips.

"If you're free tonight I'd like to take you out to dinner. Plus, I saw something at a lingerie booth back there that I think will look damn good on you. How about I get it boxed up and bring it with me when I pick you up tonight?" Noble had also seen a diamond-studded thong that would look hot on Kiki, and he planned to get one of those boxed up too.

Zsa Zsa licked her lips. She knew what time it was, and a long night with Noble Browne was just what she needed. Since she lived with her aunt, she knew they would end up staying at Noble's crib, and she had been dying to get up in that joint and finish a few things she had started.

"Sounds good, baby," she giggled. Anticipating the dick down she was guaranteed to get, and scheming on the little caper she planned to pull once he was fast asleep, was gonna keep her mind busy for the rest of the day. "Yeah, baby. That sounds real good."

10

Not only had Noble cut his date short with Zsa Zsa, if he planned to make it over to the projects for the community meeting with Sissy, then he was gonna have to dip out early on Malisha too.

"Trey did real good with his music lesson today," Noble told her as he strapped the four-year-old into the custom car seat that he had commissioned an old friend from college to design. He'd been driving Malisha and Trey to two of the boy's three music lessons every week, and he loved spending time with them. "He's making progress, baby. For real. I can see it."

Malisha smiled.

Just watching the way Noble handled her baby made her heart feel warm. Besides Jamel, there'd been no other man in the boy's life to give him a masculine touch, or to care for him like a son.

"I just hope I can keep the lessons going," Malisha stated.

"They're kinda expensive, but without them he'll just go back into a shell."

Noble nodded. "I hear you. You've gotta keep him playing that piano. It's crazy how he just knows how to hit the right notes like that. The boy might be some kinda musical prodigy."

But I can't afford to keep paying for the lessons! Malisha wanted to scream in his face. But of course she didn't. Just like her pride wouldn't allow her to ask her friends for help after Jamel died, that same pride wouldn't allow her to ask Noble for any money. Now if he offered her some cash, that would be a whole different story. But Malisha wasn't about to ask no-body for shit. She was just trying to hold on until something good happened. And the best thing that could happen right now would be for Noble's birthday to hurry up and get here so he could tell her that she was the woman he wanted to spend the rest of his life with.

Yeah, she knew there were some other chicks out there checking for him too, but Malisha just couldn't believe some-body else would be a better fit for him. She had asked Noble to tell her exactly what he was looking for in a woman. If she just knew that, it would be easy. She would become his dream. His ideal girl.

But Noble had played her to the left. He ran her some shit about how he would know exactly what he was looking for the moment he found it. Well, what the hell was he waiting on? Some kind of sign? A vivid rainbow, a four-leaf clover, or the finger of God to point him in the right girl's direction?

Malisha was terrified that something bad would happen to Noble before he was able to marry her. Jamel had died without any life insurance, and she and Trey had been left ass-out. They'd be ass-out again if Noble messed around and got hit by a damn truck or slipped on a banana peel or something while he was out there playing in traffic all day! That job of his was dangerous, and until Malisha had his signature on a marriage license she was gonna worry about his health and well-being and have a whole lotta sleepless nights!

Things had been far less stressful when she had married Jamel. She'd found out she was pregnant on a Wednesday, and by the following Monday they'd had their little low-key wedding planned. Malisha wasn't looking to have no grand, outlandish wedding with Noble, even though she knew he had crazy money and could afford it.

With a three-story brownstone all to himself, and those two luxury vehicles parked outside his crib, Noble was doing more than okay for himself. Matter fact, he was doing so good that Malisha's friends had wondered if he was a dirty cop or taking kickbacks or something under the table. Of course she had never mentioned Noble's huge stash of gold, but Malisha *was* quick to tell everybody that she had never seen a speck of grime on his personality, and that she'd never once caught Noble in a lie.

Nah, as far as Malisha could tell, Noble Browne was exactly the man he presented himself to be. He was strong and dedicated and sexy as hell. Getting past his leg was becoming a little bit easier. They didn't have sex very often, but when they did, Noble's back was so strong and he dicked her with such deep tenderness and passion that Malisha just closed her eyes and refused to think about his missing leg.

Noble had a pair of working man's hands, and Malisha loved the way it felt when he ran his rough hands up and down her body. He said she had the prettiest skin in the world, and he loved to massage her and touch her everywhere. And Malisha was all for it. She knew she was alive when Noble's coarse hands moved all over her flesh. Her nipples would tingle as he stroked her thighs, and her pussy would fill up with all the pent up juices stored inside her that were just dying to flow.

Malisha had a round, fluffy ass and she didn't mind letting Noble hit it from the back the way he liked it. But when he asked her how she wanted it, she always wanted him in her mouth. There was something real sexy about the way a man's dick felt nestled against her tongue, and Malisha had always wondered if she was a freak for enjoying head so much.

And Noble had a lot of head to enjoy too. That dick! Oh, that dick!

Not only was it thick and rugged, the control Noble had over that thing was amazing. It was like a well-trained pet. It did whatever he told it to do, and lasted as long as he wanted it to.

Malisha had surprised him by going down on him one night as they lay in bed together. She had planned to hold herself back, but something just came over her as they twisted and turned, rubbing against each other. They had gotten all worked up by their foreplay and she just had to get a taste of what he was holding.

And for real, as soon as the fat head of his pole touched the tender spot at the back of her throat, Malisha knew she had struck gold. His dick was delicious. The sweetest she had ever tasted. She tightened her lips around his shaft, as the throbbing veins vibrated against her skin turning her straight the fuck out.

Malisha had slurped that thang half to death. She didn't even blink when Noble lost his head and grabbed her cheeks and started mouth-fucking her. He pounded that dick deep into her mouth like he was really in her pussy. He had even flipped her over on her back and hovered over her, shaking the bed with his frantic thrusts as Malisha opened her mouth wide and invited him to get all down in her throat.

She had lain there in pure bliss, squeezing her legs together and sending sweet sparks through her clit as his heavy balls banged against her chin. And the moment she felt his hot cum skeet out and scald her tender throat, Malisha had lost it too. Crushing her clit between her thighs, she reached up and clenched his ass and thrust him so far down her throat that she was forced to breathe through her nose.

Malisha gave him up reluctantly when he finally slipped his limp dick out of her mouth. She licked her lips and sighed as his delicious taste lingered on her tongue. Yeah, all chicks knew how much a man liked getting him some head. But Malisha was one of the rare chicks who liked giving it just as much.

She sighed as she remembered feeling so thoroughly well-fucked when her pussy had never even been penetrated. There was more than one way to skin a cat. And she could tell by the way Noble had shook and moaned long after she was through sucking that her cat had been well-skinned.

11

Van Dyke Projects hadn't changed much over the years. Noble had known better than to roll up in the cut flossin his Corvette, so he'd cruised into Brownsville on a hog motorcycle he'd refurbished while recovering from his amputation.

His Aunt Cathy lived on the tenth floor of a fourteen-story project building. A public library sat on one side of the building, and every few minutes the El train passed by on the other side of the building. Noble looked around as he entered the lobby. His perfected swagger gave no hint to the prosthetic leg he walked on, nor to the heightened sense of alert he was on, but his street senses could pick up foul shit in the environment like a fine-tuned radar. Not only had Noble grown up hanging out in crime holes like this, he'd done a lot of undercover work in the projects too, and he knew that in this hood, every unfamiliar face walking the streets was prey.

Noble paused outside his aunt's door. Sissy lived in the apartment adjacent to Aunt Cathy's, and Noble could reach out and knock on both doors at the same time. But when his aunt's door opened to his knock, it was Sissy who greeted him.

"You made it!" she said, her pretty dimples going deep in her cheeks as she stepped back to let him in.

"Yeah," Noble said. He took a deep breath as he entered a home he had once loved and enjoyed.

The passage of time was obvious, and Aunt Cathy hadn't kept up with any type of fashion. Everything was neat and clean. The living room sofa was the same one Noble remembered from his youth, and had been preserved with plastic slipcovers. The old hi-fi sat next to it, and a heavy wooden table was pushed against the wall. Above it was a large framed photo that Noble hadn't seen in years.

It was his mother.

"Your aunt is in the kitchen," Sissy said, and led the way.

Noble followed with old memories making his chest tight. Aunt Cathy and his mother had been adopted sisters. They were a year apart in age, and neither one of them had known their real families, so they had been very close to each other. Noble had been too young when his mother died to remember anything about her, but between his father and Aunt Cathy they had kept her close and familiar in Noble's heart.

The woman sitting at the kitchen table brought a huge smile to Noble's face.

"Is that my peanut?" she shrieked at the sight of the six-foot-six boy that she had helped raise to be a man. "Is that my *peanut*? Is that my boy?"

"Is that my tauntie?" Noble chanted, playing their old familiar game as he dropped to his good knee and took her in his arms. "Is that my *tauntie*? Is that my girl?"

Tears were in both their eyes as they embraced and the old woman smacked kisses all over Noble's face.

Sissy stood quietly off to the side while Noble and his aunt hugged and got caught up. When Noble finally sat down at the table she served him and his aunt some cookies she had baked and a glass of iced tea.

"I'm sorry I haven't been by in a while, Tauntie," Noble said. He didn't tell her that the undercover work he had done in this hood woulda put her in harm's way had he been seen coming to her crib, but his aunt brushed his apology away. "I know I should have called."

"Don't never be sorry about nothing, Peanut. You hear? Besides, my phone done been cut off a few times so you couldn't have reached me anyway. We can't do nothing about what's lost. We just gotta make good use of what we have today."

Noble hung out with his aunt while he and Sissy waited for the community meeting to start. His aunt had always been a feisty thing, and as an adult Noble could really appreciate all the time and care she had taken with him over the years. Bam had never remarried. He'd remained dedicated to the bond he'd had with his wife, and he had never once been with a woman in Noble's presence. Tauntie had been the only female in young Noble's life, and it was her who had told him about the circumstances of his mother's death.

Noble watched the way Sissy moved around his aunt's kitchen. He could tell she was comfortable and knew exactly where everything was.

"Looks like Sissy is a lot of help, Tauntie. I'm glad you haven't been over here all by yourself."

His aunt nodded. "Yes, that girl is a wonder. She's always

into something in here. Cooking, cleaning up, making sure all my bills get paid. She's so good, it done got to the point where I can't find nothing. And she does the same thing for the rest of the old folks in the building. She's like a little manager. Just done took over for us. Bless her heart."

Noble looked at Sissy with mad respect and appreciation in his eyes. She was still young and beautiful. She didn't have to be stuck up in these projects fooling around with no old people, but she did it anyway. He could still see a trace of the sexy young vixen from high school in her eyes, but there was also a mature, foxy woman with a good heart in there too. A woman Noble wanted to spend a little quality time with and get to know better.

The community meeting was over an hour away, and Noble had wanted to do some grocery shopping for his aunt while he was there. Sissy showed him where his aunt kept her shopping cart, and Noble took it from the closet and headed out to shop on Livonia Avenue. Noble had gotten a grocery list from his tauntie, and Sissy had a list of her own for herself and her uncle.

"Do you remember Yardley Green from Marcus Garvey? He owns that store down the block called Green's Groceries?" Sissy asked as they walked.

"Oh yeah," Noble nodded quickly. "Yard's my boy. We went to school together. I used to chill at his store all the time when I was out here working undercover. Yard used to look out for me a lot when I was working narcotics. He was one of the few dudes around here that I could always trust."

"Oh, I didn't know y'all was tight like that."

Noble nodded again. "Yeah, we tight as hell. We hang out almost every weekend. Remember, me, Yard, and Pap was a crew back in high school. We called ourselves 'Three the Hard Way.' Yard's about to get married soon. He just called me up and invited me to his bachelor party."

Sissy cut her eyes at him. "Bachelor party? Yeah, I knew he was getting married, but he didn't tell me about no bachelor party!"

Noble laughed. "That's 'cause you're not invited!"

Sissy laughed with him, then said, "Well, I work the cash register at Yard's store a couple of nights a week, so that's where I usually shop." Sissy shook her head as they strolled down the street looking like a couple. "Yard has the lowest prices around here, but his products just ain't all that great."

"What's wrong with my man's stuff?"

Sissy shrugged. "Nothing's wrong with it, it's just that he doesn't have the biggest or the freshest selection around here. I mean, the milk and bread and eggs and stuff like that are okay, but you know you can't get no decent fresh fruits or good cuts of meat in no corner store."

"So let's go where the selection is bigger. Let's hit that supermarket over by the Chinese restaurant," Noble suggested. And then he asked as they crossed the street, "Other than going to nursing school and working for Yard, what else have you been doing with yourself? I know you're working at the hospital now, and running things for everybody in the building, but what do you do when you're not doing all that?"

Sissy shrugged. "I do stuff. . . . I like to read. I hang out with a few of my girls. Do you remember Val Boykins from Jeff?"

Noble nodded casually. Val was hot. He'd actually gotten some of that back in the day.

"Well, her sister Shannie is still around, and me and her are real cool. We chill together a lot."

Noble remembered Shannie too. She had been one of them real hard-looking chicks who threw her rap down on other females and walked around holding her imaginary nuts.

"What else you do?" he asked. "Are you with somebody? You got a man?"

Sissy looked up at him with the niggah-please face. "I ain't got time for no man. Besides, I don't need no man. Men always seem to get me in trouble."

And then she switched it up.

"How about you? I know you must have a woman somewhere. You always had a bunch of girls running behind you back in high school. I'm sure that hasn't changed."

"Nah," Noble said, defending himself. "High school and now are two different things. All of us have lived some and learned some. We ain't the same now as we were back then."

Sissy quickly agreed. "You're right about that. I can't believe all the wild shit I did in high school. I was outta control. Just wild. And stupid as hell too. But like you said, we're all different now. So," she said, bringing her question back home, "where's your girlfriend?"

Noble kept it tight.

"I don't have just a girlfriend. There are a few women that I have deep feelings for, but I'm not looking for a girlfriend. I'm trying to find a wife."

Sissy stopped in her tracks.

"A wife? You're getting married?"

Noble laughed. "Yeah, one day. My pops is sick. I wanna get married and have a tyke while he's still around."

"So, when's the big day?"

"I don't know that yet," Noble admitted. "But I'm gonna propose to somebody on my birthday. That's the day I'll get engaged."

"Wow," she said. "When's your birthday?"

"Next month," Noble answered. "On the fifteenth."

At the cash register, he let Sissy put her stuff up on the belt first. But before the cashier could finish ringing her up, Noble had slid the grocery separator to the side and told the young girl to ring up everything together so he could pay for it.

"Thanks," Sissy said to him as they walked slowly down the sidewalk passing Tilden Projects. "I appreciate it, but you didn't have to buy my stuff."

Noble nodded as he pulled the cart behind him. A slight smile was playing on his lips as he watched her walk beside him. Sissy was fine. Her waist was tight, and the jeans she wore couldn't hide what the girl was holding. Her package looked good. Not like a hot teenager, but like a fully-grown woman.

"It's no big thing," Noble said, shrugging it off. The few dollars he'd spent in the store didn't come close to matching up with what Sissy had been doing for people like his aunt. Noble was grateful to her, and he wanted to do her a solid in some kinda way too.

"Hey," he said suddenly. "I know the community meeting is about to start soon, but are you busy later on tonight? Can I take you to dinner?"

Sissy shook her head. "Sorry, after the meeting I'm getting with some people from the neighborhood watch team. I'll be sitting in the lobby from five to seven."

"Can I sit down there with you?"

Sissy laughed. "No. You have to be a team member to take a shift."

"Cool. I'll join the team, and we can go to dinner when we're done. Who do I need to talk to? Where do I sign up. Who's in charge?"

Sissy laughed again and put her warm hand on his arm. "Who's in charge, Noble? Why, that would be me."

12

Sitting on Neighborhood Watch with Sissy had been fun, and dinner at an Italian restaurant downtown had been even better. Noble knew he was playing his time kinda close. And after sitting downstairs with her for two hours, he'd put Sissy on the back of his motorcycle and cruised back to his crib to change clothes and get the whip so he could take her out to dinner in style. After dinner he planned to drive Sissy home, then zip over to see his sweet little Zsa baby.

"What's in the box?" Sissy asked as he opened his trunk and placed the gift-wrapped box containing the lingerie he'd bought for Zsa Zsa inside.

"It's a gift," Noble said. He'd made sure not to get it mixed up with the thong he'd bought for Kiki.

"For a girl?"

He nodded. "Yeah. For a very special girl."

They'd driven downtown to Campanato's, and Noble had eaten some vegetarian spaghetti while cracking Alaskan king crab legs for Sissy and piling the sweet meat high on her plate.

While they ate, they talked about Noble getting shot and losing his leg, and Sissy's decision to become a nurse, and how hard it had been for her to get into a decent school after coming out of prison.

"Being locked up was a wake-up call for me," Sissy admitted. "I learned to love myself while I was in prison. And I also learned that all the dudes I thought I had loved were just substitutes for what I really needed. For the kind of love I had been denying myself and running away from."

Noble could dig it. He had chased a lot of girls too, and the kind of love he was looking for right now was the kind his pops had shared with his mother. The kind that lasted way beyond the grave.

Noble was really enjoying himself, and he knew Sissy was talking some real shit. And it wasn't just because of the words coming outta her mouth. Nah, the girl sitting across the table from him was very different from the hot banga Sissy from his memories. But as much as he dug getting to know her again, it was just about time for Noble to dip, because he wasn't about to break his word to Zsa Zsa.

Noble drove Sissy home, and even though she kept telling him it wasn't necessary, he walked her inside the building and took her upstairs to her door.

"She's probably asleep, huh?" he asked, angling his head toward Tauntie's door.

Sissy nodded quickly. "Oh yeah. She's an early bird. She gets in the bed before eight o'clock. But I have the key if you want to go inside for something."

Noble shook his head, then kissed her on the cheek. "Nah. I don't need nothing outta there. I already put my cell number on the refrigerator, and I left her some money to pay her phone bill. *And* I promised her that from now on I'd be calling and coming by on the regular."

Thirty minutes later Noble pulled up outside Zsa Zsa's crib. She lived with her aunt on the first floor of an apartment building and all her lights were on. Noble could hear the music coming out of her windows, and he grinned as he took the boxed negligee from his trunk and tucked it under his arm.

Tonight was gonna be a good night because Zsa Zsa never disappointed. And it wasn't just the sex either, 'cause Noble coulda gotten good sex anywhere, and pussy would never be a determining factor in choosing a woman to mate with for life.

Nah. There was so much more to his Zsa baby than her exotic beauty and her bouncing ass. Zsa had charisma. She had flava and she had drive. She was ambitious and goal oriented, and people from all walks of life were naturally attracted to her. Zsa was the type of woman Noble would trust to raise his daughter or his son. She knew the streets like the back of her hand, and she could be hood at times, but she was also a softie at heart, and that was exactly what Noble liked about her. Life would be exciting and high-post with Zsa Zsa. There would never be a dull moment. She'd be a good New York City mother, and an even better New York City wife.

"Thirsty?" Zsa Zsa opened the door holding out a large carton of Tropicana orange juice. Noble grinned. He loved his orange juice. She'd gotten his favorite kind too. The one with lots of pulp. Zsa Zsa was straight thoughtful like that. Whenever he came over she made sure there was something waiting for him that he really, really liked.

And tonight he was really, really liking his Zsa baby.

He wanted to laugh as she snuck him past her aunt, who had fallen asleep in the living room chair with the television on. Zsa made him take off his shoes and creep, but Noble didn't know how the old lady could hear him walking if she was able to sleep through the loud reggae music Zsa Zsa was blasting.

"Oh, she knows what men steps sound like." Zsa Zsa laughed after they made it safely into her bedroom and closed the door. "Trust me," she said. "I had to give her some Tylenol PM because otherwise she woulda been all over you. She used to work in a group home full of fast-ass teenagers, and not one of them got pregnant on her watch." Zsa Zsa shook her head and laughed again. "My girl be on it! She can sleep through a marching band blasting up in here. But let a dude try to creep into a bedroom. She'll sit right up and tell you which way he went!"

Noble looked around Zsa Zsa's room. It belonged to a fashion designer, all right. It was decorated in silver, black, and royal purple. She had design sketches stuck all over her walls, and next to her sewing table stood a life-sized mannequin with tits and an ass that was shaped just like Zsa's. The mannequin was wearing the latest dress Zsa had designed, and it looked like she had been putting her final touches on it here and there.

"Yo," Noble said, shaking his head. "I love you and everything, Zsa baby. But your room is mad little. Besides, we too grown to be sneaking around in your aunt's house and hoping we don't get caught."

Noble wanted to add that if she wasn't so damn nosy and didn't snoop around his shit and try to pry info outta him all the time, they could be laying up in his tight crib in luxury and privacy. But he was keeping Zsa on a real long leash. Her conduct had been poor. She had to earn her way back into the bat cave, and so far she hadn't done that yet.

"Relax," Zsa Zsa told him. She pushed him down on a sofa that was covered with scraps of fabric and sat on his knee, flirting with him. "Ain't nothing wrong with sneaking a little something every now and then. You know, the thought of getting caught in the act is one of my hottest fantasies. What's yours?"

Noble groaned and slid his hands over her round hips.

"I can show you better than I can tell you," he said, tugging at the bottom of her shirt. Zsa Zsa lifted her arms and let him pull her top over her head. She shook her hair out and her bold brown titties jiggled, her pretty nipples stiffening in the cool air.

"You got it," Noble muttered, his lips reaching for one of her perfect, juicy breasts. "You got it all."

A woman like Zsa brought out the animal instincts in Noble. There were very few chicks who could go bang for bang with him the way Zsa Zsa did. Most women just wanted to be stroked and cuddled and handled with kid gloves, but not Zsa. His baby liked it hard and heavy. Like he was about to give it to her.

He inched her zipper down and licked his lips as she wriggled out of her jeans. Her thong was elegant and sexy, and her triangle was sweet-smelling and neatly trimmed. Noble pressed his nose into her navel, then opened his mouth and raked his teeth over her skin. He trailed his chin downward until he reached her chocolate patch, then he pulled the flimsy hot pink material aside and buried his face in her honey.

Zsa Zsa panted and squealed as Noble rotated his face in

her pussy. He slathered her clit and lapped up her juices, his curling, winding tongue everywhere all at once. Taking soft little slurps from her bubbling fountain, Noble cupped Zsa's ass with both hands and squeezed her soft, perfect buns. He moved her hips in his preferred motion, and Zsa Zsa gladly relinquished control and went with his flow.

Rising to his feet, Noble ripped the thong straight off her body. Zsa Zsa never blinked as he let it fall to the floor and pulled her into his arms. He nudged her until he had turned her around, then he pressed down on her shoulders, urging her to bend over the edge of the couch.

With both knees spread, Zsa Zsa backed her bold ass up high, and braced her elbows down low to support herself. Holding his dick in one hand, Noble inched it between her thick brown cheeks, teasing her asshole before swiping it down low and plunging into her pussy. Holding tightly to her hips, he fucked her slowly and gently at first, giving her body time to adjust to his presence.

But once he felt her insides loosen up, he went for it the way they both liked it. Noble plundered that sweet pussy. He deliciously abused it. Zsa Zsa's hair was strewn above her head, and she was slobbering and talking gibberish all over her fabric swatches as her man fed her with his long stick of dick.

And she gave it back to him with equal force. She bucked back hard, swallowing his dick between the mounds of her ass. She took advantage of her long-dicked man, swinging her hips in all directions and twisting and turning so he could hit it from opposite angles.

Noble's hands slid up her body and found the soft creases below her breasts. He cupped her naked flesh in his palms, weighing them like ripe fruit. He drilled her pussy like an electric jack, rubbing and squeezing her nipples until Zsa came, and came hard. She shrieked into the sofa cushions as his nut caught fire and rumbled around like an inferno in his balls.

"I'm cumming!" Noble shouted, not giving a fuck if her aunt woke up and busted them ass-naked. He slammed his dick up in her extra hard. One. Two. Three! And then he just melted, his hot seed flowing from him like a burst dam and filling the rubber with the thousands of babies he hoped to one day implant in the woman he loved.

It was a minute before either of them could talk. And as usual, it was crazy Zsa Zsa who spoke first.

"Hey, Noble," she giggled, her face still pressed down in the creases of the sofa, her beautiful ass still high in the air. "You thirsty, baby? You want some orange juice?"

13

Noble went to the gym and got in a workout on Sunday morning, then came home and soaked in a hot tub of water for most of the afternoon. Later that night, he met up with his manz Yard and Pap to shoot a little pool.

"Yo," Noble told Yard as he racked up and got ready to play. "I was on ya terrain the other day, man."

"That right?" Yard said, tipping up his beer.

Noble nodded. "I was with Sissy, man. We went grocery shopping for my aunt. Why you didn't tell me she was working for you like that?"

Yard shrugged. "What was there to tell, man? I helped her out with a few hours here and there when she needed some extra change, that's all. I didn't know she was on your mind like that."

"She wasn't," Noble said, aiming his cue and cracking the rack. "Until the other day."

Noble hung out late with his boys, and since Monday was a holiday, he decided to ask Kiki if she wanted to take the kids to Six Flags amusement park. She suggested they stay in Jersey overnight and drive home early the next morning, so Noble went online and booked two rooms at a real nice hotel, then picked up his crew and drove them down to Jersey in his freshly detailed SUV.

Owning a small business required a lot of time and work, and it had been rare for Noble's father, Bam, to find time for a whole lotta frivolous outings with his son. Noble knew how important it was for a kid to have an opportunity to do nothing but play, and he was happy to be able to take Kiki's kids out for the day.

Kiki's kids were the bizz. Her little girl was tall and lanky and loved arm wrestling and climbing all over Noble, while her son was on the quiet side and enjoyed reading the comic books that Noble took him to buy almost every weekend.

Noble had a true thing for children, and since two of the three women who could potentially become his wife were already mothers, he was careful about how he would fit into their lives. He didn't wanna make no mistakes. Any child he became a father to was gonna be treated with the utmost love and respect. The same way Bam had always treated him. Whether the kid was biologically Noble's or not wasn't gonna make a damn bit of difference neither. Yeah, he wanted his own kids too, but he was also man enough to be a father to a kid who needed one. And it was easy for people to assume that Kiki's kids were his. Their father was obviously black, and since the kids looked biracial, people just figured they were a family whenever they hung out.

Noble had treated everybody to franks, ice cream, popcorn, and candy, and he was coming off a wild roller-coaster ride with little Matt when he realized that Kiki was standing near the exit crying.

"Hey, baby," he said tenderly as he stared into her eyes and then pulled her into his arms. Kiki was sweet, but she was also strong, and Noble knew if she was crying, then some shit had to be bad. "What's wrong?" he asked, holding her close. "What happened, Ki? Tell me what's wrong?"

"*N-n-n-nothinggg!*" she wailed. Her nose had turned red and her blue eyes were full of tears. "N-n-nothing is wrong, Noble," she said, tucking her head between his shoulder and his cheek. Her hair felt like silk as it brushed against his arm.

"Everything is just so *right,*" she sniffled. She wiped her nose with the back of her hand. "I don't know. Something just came over me. Seeing you with Matt blew my mind. Every-thing is just so *right.*"

Noble stroked her hair and patted her face and let her cry it out. He made some soothing noises but he didn't have no words for her. He hadn't wanted to go on that damn roller coaster with Matt in the first place, but the boy had looked up at him with cold hope in his eyes when he asked him to take him on, and Noble didn't see where he had a choice.

And now, if it meant that much to Kiki to see him and her son together on a roller coaster, then Noble was glad he'd taken the boy. Outta all the chicks in his life, Kiki was the easiest to please. She wasn't the demanding type, and the simplest shit brought out extreme gratitude in her. She was like a puppy. Trustworthy and loyal to the bone. Noble liked that about her. She wasn't gonna be no high maintenance wifey. She would bake cookies and all that domestic shit for the kids, and she would freak him half to death at night. Kiki was easy to love.

Later that evening, after they'd left footprints over damn near every square inch of the park and ridden on almost every ride, Noble took his little family out to eat at a buffet restaurant that Matt had picked out. He watched as Kiki took her time choosing healthy foods for the kids, piling their plates up with fruits and vegetables, then letting them choose their own desserts when they were through eating. Those kids were lucky to have Kiki for their mother, Noble thought as he watched her help little Tricia pour chocolate syrup all over her ice cream.

He couldn't help digging the way Kiki's ass moved when she walked, though. Like there was a tsunami tryna get outta her drawers. It was the same way she moved when she was freaking him in private. Kiki gave the best lap dances Noble had ever received. Her body was tight and swole, and her pale skin was smooth and damn near flawless. He didn't know how a naive little white girl like her had learned to slink her hips and rock her pelvis the way Kiki did, but it was mad. Noble liked to grip her waist as she slithered like a sexy little snake in his lap, and there were times when he could barely hold his nut long enough to get inside her before he lost his head and exploded just from her moves.

He couldn't wait to get Kiki back to that hotel tonight. He had some shit planned for her, for real. He noticed she'd been guzzling crazy five-hour energy drinks all day long, and she might need to chug down a few more if she was gonna keep up with him tonight.

Sex with Kiki was more than just a physical thang. It was an emotional adventure. Kiki was the type of woman Noble wanted to make love to every single night. She was giving and creative, always trying to understand his sexual fantasies and make them come true.

Yeah, Noble thought. They had two rooms reserved, and as soon as they put the kids down for bed, him and Kiki were gonna go in the other room and use that shit up. He couldn't wait to feel her body next to his. He just couldn't understand how she was so good at making all his dreams come true.

There was something special about Kiki.

Something very special that Noble never wanted to let go.

14

It was Wednesday and Noble rushed home after work so he could change clothes and jet across town to pick up Malisha and Trey. On the way there he made a quick stop at Radio Shack, where he purchased a pair of those new headphones that had just been put out by Dr. Dre. The kid behind the counter showed him their low, medium, and high-priced sets, and even though Trey was just a tyke, Noble said fuck it and bought the boy the best quality pair they had, which cost him just over three bills.

Malisha was waiting at the door when he pulled up, and he couldn't help the big grin that spread over his face at the sight of her. This mami was pure class. Goodness just radiated from her. She damn near had a halo floating over her head. Noble liked the way her short, layered hairstyle framed her face. She looked relaxed. Fresh and neat. Her makeup light but fashionable, her clothes screamed with ladylike grace. Bottom line, Malisha's shit was always well put together.

And her body. Damn. It was a baby-maker, for real. Noble

could spend hours just rubbing her feet, legs, ass, and arms, because Malisha had the sweetest, softest cinnamon brown skin he had ever touched. Noble respected dedication and honesty, and Malisha had a whole lot of both. She had devoted herself to making sure her son got the best treatment possible. And unlike some of the other single moms Noble had dated in the past, there wasn't a scheming bone in Malisha's body. What you saw was exactly what you got with that girl, and her integrity alone was a big turnon for Noble.

Noble thought about the mind-boggling diamond he was about to put on somebody's finger. It was important to him that his choice in a woman was sound and based on good judgment. A woman couldn't always have her hand held out. Sometimes she had to wanna look out for her man too, and Malisha was the good-looking-out type. Noble couldn't count how many times she'd rushed outta the bank and walked to the corner to check on him.

And when Noble needed somebody, he knew exactly who to call. When it was cold outside Malisha would brave that hawk and bring him steaming cups of hot cocoa, and in the summer Noble was always happy to look up and see her sashaying toward his grid box with a sweet smile and a tall cup of icy lemonade.

Shit, let him cough or sneeze. That girl would be right there, hovering over him like a little mother hen. She'd show up outta nowhere with cough syrup, Tylenol, and lemon honey tea.

Yeah, Malisha was all about taking care of the man in her life, and Noble knew she'd be the type of wife who would stand by him through thick or thin, sickness or health. It wouldn't have mattered to her if Noble had lost both his damn legs. A keeper like Malisha woulda simply dedicated her life to pushing him around in his wheelchair.

In fact, it had been Malisha who Noble had leaned on when Bam first took sick. When Noble got the call that his father had been rushed to the hospital and was in critical condition, Malisha had found a babysitter for Trey, and actually got to the hospital before Noble did.

"How is he?" Noble had asked her the moment the elevator doors opened on the intensive care unit. Malisha had been staring through the hospital glass with extreme worry in her eyes.

"I don't know, baby," she'd said, putting her arms around him and holding him tight. "The doctor was just here, but he wouldn't tell me anything. Let's go find him now."

Minutes later, Malisha was right by his side as the doctor explained that Bam had a terminal condition that would eventually take his life. As he listened to the doctor, Noble had been stunned into numbness. It was one of the few times that he had wobbled on his fake leg, and he had thanked God that Malisha was there to support him and hold him up.

Matter of fact, it was Malisha who had had the presence of mind to bring up Bam's estate, and to remind Noble that he would need a power of attorney from his father if something went wrong.

"It happens all the time at the bank," she explained. "A husband or wife, or parent or child will have a bank account full of money, but when they die their loved ones aren't able to get a dime. Everything has to go through the probate court. Unless, of course," she added, "you take care of business while your loved one is still alive."

As savvy as Noble was in his investments, he had never considered what would happen to Bam's money when his father died. Shit, he had never thought about what would happen to him if his pops wasn't in his life no more. Just the thought of losing the best thing he'd ever had in life got Noble real shook.

"I don't know if I'm on my pop's accounts," he admitted. "I've never needed his money. I've always had my own."

"Well, don't worry," Malisha had assured him. "The doctor says his disease progress is relatively slow. Once he's out of the hospital we'll make sure all his papers are in order."

Malisha had squeezed his hand gently, then asked, "But what about you, Noble? You don't have any blood relatives besides your father. What would happen to all your money if you suddenly died?"

Noble could only shake his head. Malisha was right. His tauntie wasn't related by blood, and Bam was all he had. Without a wife and kids, who was gonna get all the gold and securities he had worked so hard to earn? The fucked up state of New York? Hell nah.

"I don't know," he admitted. "I always thought I'd have me a tyke or two to leave my shit to when I passed."

"Well, don't worry about it right now," Malisha had said. "But it's something to think about. In fact, if you want I can hold a copy of your safety deposit key just so you know somebody has it. It's not something most people do unless they're married, but since you don't have a family—yet—it's something you might wanna think about."

Malisha had been right. Noble hadn't given up his key, but

over the past few months he had been thinking about it. He'd been thinking hard. And since his birthday was almost right around the corner, he needed to make a good decision, fast.

"Hi, handsome." Malisha greeted him with a smile and a kiss as he walked in the door. She was wearing a sexy little green dress and Noble took her in his arms and let his hands circle her small waist.

"Wus good, mami?" he muttered, his lips nuzzling that sweet caramel spot right above her collarbone. As hard as Noble tried to juggle his women and keep each of them satisfied, his interactions with Malisha were never based on sex. It was hard for her to stay all night at his crib, and it wasn't easy going out because of Trey's limited mobility, so Noble brought dinner over and they ate in a lot. They read together, watched a lot of movies, and made heart connections even when their bodies never touched.

Malisha was especially hyped today, and excitement danced in her eyes as she kissed Noble's lips, then threw her hands high in the air. "Only two more weeks till your birthday! I'm so excited, baby! I'm gonna get you the very best birthday present ever!"

Noble laughed inside. A lot of people had promised him great gifts for his birthday, but on his special day it was him who was gonna be the giver. The giver of an icy-sweet ten-carat engagement ring!

The studio where Trey took his music lessons was high-post and state of the art. Noble knew it probably cost Malisha a gwap to enroll her son at an uptown joint like this, but for what they offered, it was worth it. They had soundproof rooms and all kinds of audio equipment and equalizers. The area where the musical instruments were displayed was straight laid out.

They were walking past the front counter when the receptionist called Malisha's name.

"Ms. Chambers!" The redheaded older woman waved her over.

Noble wheeled Trey and followed Malisha to the counter.

"How's it going today, Trey?" the older woman cooed as she came from behind the counter to greet Trey. The little boy's expression never changed as she cupped his cheeks and smoothed his hair. "Where's your beautiful smile?"

"He's doing great," Malisha answered, "but he's not all that responsive right now. I'll stop him back by your desk after his lesson. He'll be smiling and laughing like crazy after that."

The older woman glanced at Noble, then back at Malisha.

"Umm, Mr. and Mrs. Chambers," she began.

"Oh!" Malisha cut in. "We're not married yet. Noble isn't Trey's father. But we'll be engaged in a couple of weeks—" She caught herself. "*Possibly* engaged in a couple of weeks, though."

"Really?" the woman said. "I had no idea you weren't already married." She flashed Noble a smile of approval and said, "He takes such good care of your son when he's here, and he handles him so gently and with so much love. . . . I just assumed only a father would behave that way."

Malisha grinned and leaned into Noble's arm.

"He's gonna be a great father. I can already tell. Our kids won't miss out on anything. They won't ever have to work. They'll be set for life."

"Speaking of missing out," the woman said as her voice dropped low, "we wouldn't want Trey to miss out on any lessons but . . . the credit card we have on file for you was declined for payment. I tried to run it three times, but each time it came back the same way."

Malisha's smile froze on her face.

"Umm, declined?" Her eyebrows furrowed and she shook her head. "I don't know how that could have happened. I have plenty of credit." She shrugged, then smiled. "You must have my old card. That one probably expired."

"I'm sure that's what it is," the receptionist agreed. "If you give me your new card I'll try to run it again right now."

Malisha shook her head.

"I don't have it on me. It's at home. I need to activate it from my home phone. How about I call you when I get home and you can take the charge over the phone?"

The woman nodded agreeably. "That would be just fine. Just give me a call, and I'll be happy to do that for you. In the meantime," she continued, "would you like to reschedule Trey's lesson for another day?"

Malisha shook her head again.

"Why do I have to reschedule? We're already here and we drove a long way. I think Trey should be allowed to have his lesson right now, and I'll make sure you get your payment later on tonight."

Noble cleared his throat. The older lady looked embarrassed, and Malisha did too.

"If it was up to me," the lady began again, "I'd just as soon let him take his lesson. But we have specific rules here, and all lessons must be paid for in advance."

Noble stepped from behind Trey's chair and leaned on the counter.

"Here," he said, fishing his platinum American Express card from his wallet. He shrugged Malisha off when she acted like she was tryna protest. "Let me take care of this for you, baby."

"The lessons are paid for by the month," the receptionist informed him. "Sorry, that's the policy."

"No problem," Noble told her smoothly. "You can charge my credit card for the next three months."

15

About a week later Noble received a troubling phone call from his aunt.

"What's wrong, Tauntie?" he asked when he heard the worry in her voice.

"There's a fox in the chicken coop," the old lady declared. "You know that money you left for me to pay my telephone bill?"

"Yes."

"Well, somebody done stole it!" the old woman said.

"Did they break into your apartment? Were you robbed?"

"No, but my friend Julie who lives upstairs on the twelfth floor had some money stolen from her too! You a cop, right, Peanut? Well, I'ma need you to come over here and get somebody arrested!"

Noble shook his head trying to understand. There had been a string of ongoing burglaries both in his aunt's project building and the one across from her. The fried chicken joint across the way had been robbed too, and even his boy Yard's spot had been hit a few times. But there was no way somebody could have broken into his aunt's crib with her sitting right there.

Besides, Noble knew his aunt didn't like to leave the house. It had to be a real special occasion to get her to go somewhere. If somebody had jimmied her lock and stolen something from her, then she would have had to been right there to see it.

"Tauntie," he said gently, hoping to calm her down. "Nobody came in your place. You're home all the time. Maybe you just misplaced the money. Could that be it?"

The old lady huffed into the phone.

"I know where I left that money, Peanut! I swear I do! Somebody is going around here stealing, and I think I know who it is!"

"Who?" Noble asked, and when his aunt answered it was the funniest shit he had ever heard.

"It's Sissy!" she said like she really meant it. "That damned Sissy is a goddamn thief!"

Noble finally got his aunt calmed down and promised to pay her telephone bill online. As soon as he hung up from her he called Sissy to tell her what was up.

"Hey," he said, trying hard how to figure out what to say. The last thing he wanted was for Sissy to get offended by his aunt's crazy accusations and stop helping the needy people in her hood.

But Noble didn't have to worry. When he told Sissy what his aunt had said, she bust out laughing like she was taking it all in stride.

"Noble," she said, "why do you think I asked you to come

visit your aunt? I wanted you to check her out, but what I really wanted was to see if she remembered you."

"Is that right?"

"Yeah, it is. Your aunt has dementia," Sissy explained. "Just like a lot of older folks in our community do. It comes with old age, but it also comes from a lack of brain stimulation. Our old people tend to sit at home day in and day out, just looking out the window. That's what your aunt Cathy does. I noticed her forgetfulness over a year ago. It took me a while to get her to agree to see a doctor, but when she did, dementia was his diagnosis. That's why I think it's good that you're back in her life. Maybe you can help keep her memories alive for as long as possible."

Noble's heart sank at the news of his aunt's condition. His parents had been well into their forties when they had him, and his aunt was a year older than his mother. That would make her over seventy. Damn.

"Well, I'm glad you're not mad about her accusing you of stealing," he said. "I hope this won't make you stop doing the things you do for her."

"Nope," Sissy said. "It won't affect our relationship at all. I'm a nurse, Noble. I work with geriatric patients every day. Just last week an old white man at the hospital accused me of being his long-lost daughter who stole fifty-thousand dollars from under his mattress. Noble, that man was homeless before somebody brought him in off the street to get some medical care. He didn't even have fifty cents. That's just how it goes when folks get old and feeble minded. They don't mean no harm. Your aunt probably put her money someplace and forgot about it. I'll stop by there tonight and try to help her find it."

Grateful wasn't the word to describe what Noble was feeling for Sissy.

"Well, if you find it," he said, "just put it up for her. I'll pay the bill online, and that way she won't have to worry about it."

"No problem," Sissy said.

And then before she could hang up Noble blurted out real quick, "Are you busy tonight? Can we get together? You do so much for everybody else, let me do something special for you. I wanna cook dinner for you, Sissy. My place, at seven-thirty. Can you be there?"

Noble was grinning like a mothafucka when she said yes. He couldn't wait for seven-thirty to roll around. He couldn't wait to get Sissy's fine ass up in the bat cave. Yeah, he realized he only had a few days to propose to the woman who was gonna be his wife, but Noble wasn't married yet. And as sweet as Sissy was, and as bricked up as she had his drawers, he was ready to get it on!

Sissy had taken a taxi over to his crib, and for the last ten minutes Noble had been standing back as she took a tour of his entire house, except his bedroom, and oohed and ahhed at all his stuff. When she had gotten her eyes full, he led her into the kitchen, where he'd set out a restaurant-style tablecloth and some fine crystal and china that somebody had pawned at Bam's shop and never came back to get.

"I've never had a man cook dinner for me like this," Sissy admitted shyly. She picked up one of the gold forks that was part of the table setting. "Especially with nothing as nice as this." She giggled. "I almost don't know how to act."

Noble grinned. "Just act like you know, Sissy. I'm not no strange dude. We been knowing each other damn near all our lives. Be comfortable, and act like you know."

The teenaged boy in him couldn't believe that he was alone in a crib with the infamous Sissy Tarver. He almost wanted to jump up and down and call Pap and Yard over to brag on this shit, but the man in Noble knew better. He was grown enough to know the difference between a misguided teenager and a fully mature woman. All those young-head sixteen-year-old fantasies he used to have about her, he pushed them to the back of his mind and concentrated on serving her dinner.

He had stopped at a meat market and picked up a couple of quality steaks. He'd marinated them for two hours, and now they were in the oven broiling. Noble took the salad he had freshly tossed out the fridge and set it on the counter. Then he sliced a long loaf of Italian bread in half, and spread garlic butter on both sides and put that in the broiler too.

When dinner was ready he served Sissy with gold utensils. He spread a gold-trimmed white napkin across her knees and helped her push her chair closer to the table. They laughed and reminisced as they ate, and Sissy swore she had never tasted steak so tender. She made Noble write down his cooking directions so she could make it the same way at home.

"Yo, can I get you a little bit of dessert?" Noble asked when they were through eating. He had swung by Junior's and picked up a fresh-baked cheesecake. It was chilling with a bottle of wine, on a sterling silver serving cart in the sitting area of his bedroom.

Sissy shrugged. "I guess so. I'm kinda full, but if you already have something sweet I'll eat it."

"Oh, I got something sweet," Noble said softly. "But I'm serving it in my bedroom."

Sissy shook her head quickly and laughed. "Nah, that's okay. I'm old school. I'm used to eating in the kitchen."

Noble laughed too. "Cool, I respect that. But I really do have a cheesecake sitting upstairs in my room. For real. You ain't gotta go in my bedroom, Sissy. But you do have to help me eat that damn cake."

Noble kicked himself as he ran upstairs to get the cake and wine. He had to remember what he was working with. Sissy was prolly the beer and chips type. Cheesecake and wine on a five-thousand-dollar bed was prolly too much for her.

Noble told himself that he wasn't tryna push up on Sissy. He was just trying to show her some consideration for taking care of his aunt. But still . . . in the back of his mind that sixteen-year-old kid with the rock-hard dick just wouldn't shut up. It kinda hurt that after all the pussy Sissy had given out in high school, she still didn't wanna give him none.

"I know what you're thinking," Sissy said when he came back to the kitchen. She was wiping off the table, and had already scraped their plates into the garbage and rinsed them off in the sink. "You still looking at me as the Sissy you thought you knew back in high school, Noble. But I already told you, I'm not that chick no more. Almost everything about me has changed. I don't give blow jobs on the staircase no more, and hand jobs under the table are out of the question. I'm not a ho no more, Noble. I can't even tell you the last time I fucked with a man like that."

"Sissy!" Noble protested like he was indignant, although he clearly remembered one of his classmates telling him that Sissy had poured half a bottle of lotion in her palm and jacked his shit halfway to heaven. "I didn't say you was a ho! I never thought you was one neither!"

She just shrugged. She looked like she had been through this type of shit so much that it didn't even press her out no more. "It don't matter, Noble. I don't care what nobody thinks. I told you, I found out who I really was when I went to prison, and I'm good with that."

Noble had wanted to drive her home, but Sissy had insisted on taking a cab. She had put her arms around him at the door, and even kissed him on the cheek. Noble had been too ashamed to even put his arms around her, but she'd pressed up against him and given him a brief feel of what he'd been craving all these years.

"I know you, Noble. But I don't *know you,* know you. I ain't been with a dude in a good minute. Since you're back in your aunt's life we'll be seeing a lot more of each other now. Let's take it slow and see what happens. Cool?"

Noble nodded. He was glad Sissy wasn't still giving up the booty outta both her panty legs. He was feeling her even more now that she'd turned him down. He could dig where she was coming from about taking your time to let a relationship develop too, but Noble didn't have as much time as Sissy did. He was about to pop the big question in just a few days, and Noble could only hope and pray he wasn't about to make a big mistake.

16

It was two days before Noble's birthday, and him and Pap were going to their boy Yard's bachelor party. Just a few hours earlier Yard had called Noble and told him his store had been robbed again the night before.

"What's this?" Noble asked. "Five, six times?"

"Yeah, them grimy niggahs hit me again, man," Yard complained. "But I'ma get they asses this time. They about to get exposed!"

"You know who did it?" Noble asked. "Do I need to call one of my boys at the precinct and have 'em go pick somebody up?"

"Nah," Yard said. "Not yet. I put one of those hidden video cameras up in my joint a couple of weeks ago. It was rolling good and everything, but now I can't get the fuckin' tape out. I got my boy down at Best Buy working on it for me, and as soon as he gets that tape rolling I'ma smash whatever thieving niggah's face is on it!"

Noble knew Yard was serious about that shit, and in a way he missed being the kind of cop that bagged bad guys every day. Directing traffic was decent, but it wasn't what Noble wanted to do for the rest of his life. He was actually thinking about retiring and starting his own business. He had plenty of cream stashed in plenty of places, and if he never worked again, him—and whoever he decided to marry—would still be set.

Just thinking of the girl he was gonna marry put a grin on Noble's face. Yep, he had made his decision. The lucky honey had been chosen. He had picked door number . . . It had been hard as hell for him to cross all those lovely, beautiful women off his list and settle on just one, but Noble had done it. He was going to propose to his number-one honey in less than forty-eight hours, and he was more than sure that he'd be doing the right thing by taking her for his wife.

Yard's bachelor party was being held at an exclusive gentleman's club downtown. His boys had rented a private room, and had the liquor and the broads on stock in ample supply. They'd chosen to have it on a Sunday because the rates were half price, and even though everybody had to go to work the next day, Yard was set to have a big turnout.

Noble thought about the bachelor party he was gonna have one day soon. He planned to take a lot of notes at Yard's party so he could get some ideas on how he wanted his done.

He drove downtown in his 'Vette, feeling real sure about himself. He'd swung by to see Bam earlier in the day and he had been happy to see his father on his feet and feeling good. There was nothing he could do for his pops medically or financially that wasn't already being done. Bam had some of the best doctors in the city, and thanks to his knowledge of the market and their early investing habits, the old man had enough money to keep him comfortable in his final days.

All Bam was missing now was a grandchild. Noble knew he wasn't gonna get his new wife knocked up on their wedding night, but he hoped she wouldn't mind having his baby sooner rather than later.

It was close to ten when Noble arrived at the party. Pap opened the door for him and handed him a glass of yak.

"Whut up, niggah!" his boy said, slurring his words. "It's about time you got here!" A half-naked chick with butterscotch skin and gigantic titties was hanging off his arm. Pap twisted one of her two-inch nipples and bust out laughing.

Noble took the drink and dapped Pap out. His dude was already well lit, and so were most of the other guys who were chilling up in the suite. Pap nodded toward a large room to Noble's left and told him he could find Yard in there.

As he entered the room, Noble grinned and shook his head. Mad food had been catered, and sexy-ass go-go dancers and waitresses wearing heels and thongs were everywhere.

He looked for his boy and spotted Yard sitting on a king's chair with a freak perched on each knee. The two hot-body chicks were giving him a double-trouble lap dance, and his boy was so open on them strippers he had sweat dripping from his chin.

The girls were beauties, but Noble could tell they were professionals performing strictly for cash. Yard looked ready to throw both chicks on the floor and fuck the dog shit outta them, but it was hard for Noble to get turned on by a chick who shook her ass for a living. It was like being with a prostitute. You could never tell if she was feeling you for real, or just doing her damned job.

A cute little Hispanic chick had just walked by and squeezed Noble's nuts when Pap yelled for everybody to shut the fuck up because they were about to roll Yard's bachelor cake into the room.

The joint got real quiet as some funky-slow stripper music came outta the speakers, and two dudes pushed a huge round box decorated like a white wedding cake into the room. The box was sitting up on a dolly, and streams of silky white material was draped around each layer of the cake.

Pap held up his drink and was in the middle of making a dead playa's toast to Yard, when the top of the cake popped open and a stunning white chick rose up outta that bad boy like a genie coming out of a bottle.

Noble's eyes bucked open wide as she slithered and strutted and paraded her firm frame around the room for all the men to see, winding her creamy body like ten miles of smooth, delicious road.

"Take it *off*! Take it *off*! Take it *off*!" yelled the guy standing next to Noble as he waved some ho's garter belt high in the air.

Pap nudged him and screamed something in his ear, but Noble was frozen where he stood as he watched every niggah in the room get a hard-on from the solid hunk of good ass that was being shaken by the stripper. She was working her body so scrumptiously, bucking and rolling her pelvis like she was getting a damn good fucking, that it was no surprise that niggahs was starting to close in on her as she danced with her eyes closed and a smile of pure delight on her wicked, pretty face.

It wasn't until she starting inching off her diamond-studded thong and a thick mass of dudes rushed to surround her that Noble was able to move. And move he did.

Straight out the mothafuckin' door!

17

The next day Noble stood on his grid square chewing the fuck outta his whistle. It had been a long, crazy night, and he'd spent a lot of time fuming over how he had let himself get straight played.

Seeing Kiki bust outta that cake topless and wearing the diamond-studded thong he'd bought her had almost fucked him up. He'd wanted to fight his boy Pap when he'd hollered, "Yo, *No!* Man, ain't that one of the broads you tryna wife?"

Now he knew where her sleazy ass had picked up all them cold nasty tricks! Kiki was a graduate of Stripper's University, and Noble was gonna lay a charge on her scandalous ass the moment her bus pulled up at the stop.

Just the thought that he'd been considering her as a potential life mate, and as the mother of his unborn tykes, had Noble fuming. He wasn't the type of cat to get mad and fly off the handle on the regular, but fuckin' around with a shameless bitch like Kiki could make even the most peaceful brother get throwed off.

There'd been so many horny niggahs in the room last night that Noble knew Kiki hadn't seen him, and since tomorrow was his birthday, she was probably rolling around the city thinking she was still in the runnings. For all Kiki knew, she was about to get plastered with a fat engagement ring, but Noble knew better. Her ass had already been straight crossed off his list. He felt for her kids, but she was gonna have to find another sucker-niggah's pole to climb.

Noble was feeling like the biggest sucker on the block when his phone vibrated on his hip. He waited until the light turned red, then stepped outta the grid and crossed the street to the sidewalk.

He had a text from his boy Yard, and Noble narrowed his eyes as he read what it said: **Got the tape out. U ain't gonna believe who's on it. Holla.**

Noble's fingers fumbled to open up his contacts and press Yard's name, and when his dude answered the phone, Noble could tell by the tone of his voice that shit was not gonna be good.

"S'up?" he asked. "Who's on the tape?"

"Man, I didn't believe that shit when I seen it. I ain't wanna believe it, yo. It's fucked up, that's what's real, though. Ya girl been fucking me up."

Noble frowned. "Yo, what the fuck you talkin' about? *My* girl? Who? Who been fuckin' you up?"

Noble was in no way prepared for the name that Yard dropped on him.

It exploded on his head like a bomb.

"*Sissy,* niggah!" Yard spit. "Sissy's on the tape digging her fingers all in my pie! She's the one been stealing from the old folks in the building too. Her and that dyke bitch, Shannie! Man, don't you trust that girl, I'm telling you, No. That trifling bitch is a lesbo *and* a thief!"

Sissy was walking to work swinging her arms and looking all innocent when Noble spotted her. If there was one thing Noble didn't respect, it was larceny. As a kid there had been plenty of junkies and criminal-minded nigs who figured they could pull an easy kick door on Bam and make off with his money and his hocked shit, but Noble's father had always been ready for them. Bam had taught Noble that the only thing worse than a liar was a thief.

And one was coming straight at him right now.

He watched as Sissy made her way through the intersection. She was almost up on him when Noble broke.

"Yo, *bandit!*" he spit angrily. "How the fuck could you steal from all them poor old people, Sissy? My boy Yard got you on tape, miss! You better hope they don't send your ass back to jail—"

Suddenly Noble caught a glimpse of movement outta his right eye.

The bus!

It was Kiki's bus! An image of her round, naked ass bucking and popping outta that cake flashed through Noble's mind. He had some bizz to handle with that chick real quick too!

Sissy was opening her mouth to deny his charges when something whizzed between them. It was hot and fast, and the sound it made was unmistakable.

"Get down!" Noble shouted, but Sissy wasn't even trying to hear him. She took off running. In fact, she barreled right through him, wobbling him on his feet and knocking his fake leg out from under him.

Noble hit the ground hard as Sissy hauled ass. He turned his head and saw her jump on the bus that had just pulled up at the corner stop, screaming for the driver to take off.

Noble could only watch as Kiki, staring at him from the driver's seat with her big blue eyes, got hip to the flying bullets and was trying to decide whether or not to step on the gas. Noble flipped over on his belly. Bullets were zipping over his head. His prosthesis strap had slipped off his thigh and his leg was loose in his pants. Bullets were coming from both directions, and Noble knew he had to move. Pulling himself up on his good knee, he half-hopped, half-hobbled toward the idling bus for cover.

But before he could get there, he heard Sissy yelling again. *"Drive,* bitch! *Drive!"* she screamed.

Noble was only a few feet away when Kiki did just that. Their eyes locked for a split second, and then the unmistakable hiss of hydraulics sounded as the bus pulled off, leaving Noble standing in the street on one leg, exposed to the gunfire.

And he was straight exposed too. To Noble it felt like déjà vu. He was right back in that abandoned auto shop taking hot rounds all over his body. But it wasn't a drug bust gone bad this time, Noble realized. It was a bank robbery. Two security guards had chased three armed men out the front doors of Omega Bank. They were trading bullets back and forth, and Noble was caught in the crossfire.

The screech of tires and the blare of horns filled the air as the bank thieves turned and began firing back. Drivers ducked down in their seats and passengers hit the floorboards. The blind vendor at the corner newsstand went down, and the terrified screams of his wife and other pedestrians pierced the air.

Noble had always heard that lightning never struck the same place twice. But that didn't stop him from catching another heat round. A stray slug sank into Noble's thigh, and both his feet flew out from under him. Once again he was down on the ground, shot up and defenseless.

Malisha and her coworkers were staring out of the bank window as the security guards chased the three thieves into the street. In horror, she realized that Noble was ass-out in the middle of the gunfight, and when he grabbed his leg and crumpled to the ground, Malisha reacted from her gut, without thinking.

Ignoring the warnings of her coworkers, Malisha ran outta the bank screaming Noble's name. Oblivious to the danger, she rushed out into the street. But instead of pulling Noble to safety, she started patting and searching the downed man's pockets as he struggled to sit up.

"I'm okay, baby," he muttered, dazed and confused. The sound of police sirens was in the air, and three patrol cars had just pulled up on the scene. Another bullet whizzed by and Noble instinctively reached for Malisha. He thought she had rushed out to help him, but when he tried to roll his body protectively on top of hers, she reached back and smacked the shit outta him and screamed, "Don't die! Don't you *dare* fuckin' die, 'cause we ain't married yet! Those assholes hit the goddamn vault! Give me the key to the safety deposit box so I can make sure all my gold is okay!"

Noble lay back on the ground and closed his eyes.

These chicks were just too fuckin' much.

He had a feeling he was gonna be single for a long, long time.

18

The following morning Noble was discharged from the hospital on crutches. It was September fifteenth, his birthday, but Noble was feeling anything but happy.

"Yo," his boy Pap said as he was driving Noble home. Department regulations required officers who received a gunshot to be admitted overnight, and Noble was ready to go hide out in his own crib now. "You was real lucky yesterday, dude. The department's gonna get you another plastic leg, man. I saw what that hollow point did to your old one. You lucky them stupid security guards didn't take out your real leg."

Noble just nodded. He was grateful for everything that had happened to him yesterday. His prosthetic leg had been demolished, but at least his eyes had been opened. He smirked when he thought about how them scandalous chicks had tried to rush him at the hospital once the danger had passed and they found out he was okay. Well, it wasn't never gonna be okay with him.

You don't run the fuck off and leave somebody to die!

Kiki, Malisha, Zsa Zsa, and especially Sissy. Noble had put all those chickenheads up to roost. He didn't want none of them jawns nowhere around him. They were all shameful and unworthy. Tryna run game on a brothah for his riches and his jewels. That was just like a damn woman, Noble thought, shaking his head. He was through fuckin' with chicks for a good long while!

Noble's street was lined with cars when they rolled up on his block. Pap double-parked outside the brownstone and helped Noble get out.

"You got the steps, man?" he asked. "I'ma go find a parking spot right quick, then meet you inside."

Crutches were a minor thing to Noble. He'd mastered them during his rehab period while he was waiting to get fitted for his leg. He was just about to maneuver his way up when he spotted her sitting on the top stair.

"Happy birthday," she said softly. She was wearing a mean khaki dress and she looked like a dream, but Noble knew she was truly a nightmare in disguise.

"What are you doing here, Zsa Zsa? You didn't get the memo? Your application has been denied, so you might as well step off."

She stood up. "I don't know what's going on, Noble, but I don't like it. I mean, I see shit all over the news about a cop getting shot in midtown, then when I rush to the emergency room I find out my name is on some kinda access-denied list. I was worried about you, Noble! I was blowing up your phone! What the hell is going on?"

Noble smirked. "Save all that bullshit for your next mark, baby. I peeped your little conniving-ass shenanigans a long time ago." He leaned on one crutch and counted off on his fingers. "All the time snooping in my shit. Going through my fuckin' clothes, asking me all kinds of trick questions, tryna get up in my crib and crack my damn security code . . . your sticky-ass fingers been on my black panther sculpture too. *Gold digger!* I don't know why you over here today 'cause I wasn't never planning to marry you. You ain't the one. Your hood ass wasn't even in the runnings."

"*Noble!*" Zsa Zsa pleaded, and despite his anger, the look of pain on her face poked him in the heart. "Think about what you're saying, baby. I ain't never worked against you in no kinda way. All I tried to do was make you happy. I would never hurt you."

"Yeah. Cool. Then thank you. But you ain't the type of woman I can be happy with. I gotta be with somebody I can trust. And that ain't you."

Noble was just waiting for Zsa Zsa to spark off on him like the bugged little project chick she was. But instead, she surprised him by walking calmly down the steps in her little khaki dress and safari hat and strolling right past him.

"Thank you too," she turned and said, her slanted, pretty eyes shooting fire at him. " 'Cause I can't trust no dude who don't trust me."

Noble didn't bother to answer. He was done. He never even looked back as he hopped up the steps on his crutches and stood on one leg outside his front door. He had just punched in his alarm code and stuck his key in the lock when the door swung open on its own, and he got the shit shocked straight outta him.

"SURPRISE!"

A whole crew of homeys from the police department and traffic control were standing in his living room. Noble leaned on his crutches, stunned.

"Yo," he said, stepping inside slowly. Everybody was dressed crazy as hell. In safari clothes. He looked past a few people and saw his father sitting in the kitchen, and his tauntie smiling at him from her wheelchair. Bam was dressed like the Crocodile Hunter, and his aunt had on a cute little jungle hat.

"What's going on?"

"Happy birthday!" everybody screamed out. His boy Yard came up and pressed a cold can of beer into his hand, as Noble made his way over to dap his father and kiss his aunt.

He stood on one leg as the dudes came over and shook his hand, and the girls all smiled and showed him some birthday love.

Noble let two ladies from his old precinct guide him over to the couch. A couple of young girls from traffic enforcement scooted over so he could sit down.

"Where all y'all come from?" Noble asked the girl on his left. "Who broke into my crib? How'd y'all get past my security system?"

His dining table had been dragged into the front room and it was laid out with all his favorite foods. There were gifts, wrapped in jungle paper, stacked up under the table on the floor. Noble just couldn't believe it. He'd never had a surprise party in his life, and to have one on today of all days . . .

He looked around. His whole shit was decorated! In a crazy safari theme! Monkeys was swinging from vines, and lions and zebras was hanging from the ceiling. How the fuck did they know?

"For real," he nudged his girl Daydra, who sat beside him munching on a plate of hot wings and deviled eggs. "Who set all this shit up?"

Daydra laughed. "It was that crazy-ass Zsa Zsa! She's been working on us for months. She told everybody exactly what you liked, and made sure we showed up to deliver."

"Ooooh, *shit!*" Noble said as the full realization of what he'd done smacked him right upside the head.

"Did you see your cake?" Daydra asked, pointing toward the table.

Noble felt his heart drop when he saw the two-foot cake made in a replica of his favorite black panther. His long-lost sculpture was sitting on the table right beside the cake, and whoever had baked it had made it damn near identical.

Noble looked up. A handwritten banner hung above the table. It was shaped like an elephant and had a cloth draped over its back. The words on the cloth read,

NO MATTER WHO YOU CHOOSE, I HOPE ALL YOUR DREAMS COME TRUE.

Beside him, Daydra laughed again. "Yo, Noble, I hope you got a real sweet tooth because that damn Zsa Zsa went through five bakers tryna make sure your cake came out just right. It had to be a perfect match to that ugly-ass panther thingie, and somehow it is."

Noble just couldn't believe it.

"You want something to eat?" Daydra asked, holding out her plate.

But Noble jumped up so fast her food hit the floor.

He reached for his crutch but it slipped from his hand. Cursing, he hopped in a half circle, then bounded toward the front window, bumping into his party guests as he jetted across the room.

He made it over to the window and quickly peered out. His boy Pap was down there. He was leaning on a whip comforting Zsa Zsa in his arms.

"*Yo!*" Noble screamed. He flung the window up and pushed the screen straight out. "Zsa Zsa!" he yelled. "Wait, baby! I can explain!"

The look on her face hit him like a bullet, and before Noble could hobble halfway down his front steps, the woman he wanted to marry jumped in her ride, slammed the door, and sped off down the block.

19

It took mad weeks of begging before Noble finally eased up. No matter how much he called her or swung by her crib, or hit her on Facebook or went looking for her on the job, Zsa Zsa just wasn't having it.

"Yo, man," his dude Pap told him as they watched a basketball game at a wing and beer joint one night. A couple of hotties at the bar were trying to press up on Noble, but he couldn't even see them chicks. Every girl he looked at turned into Zsa Zsa. She was the only girl he wanted. "I think you was trying to do too much, homey," Pap said. "You know. Tryna figure out if you wanna be with one chick is hard enough. But having three and four on a string?" Pap shook his head and guzzled his beer. "Bad business."

Noble sighed. Pap was right. His girls mighta been scheming and tryna fuck over him, but in a way he had been fuckin' over them too. He had 'em reaching and stretching. Doing the Flava Flav thing. Competing for a relationship like a bunch of thoroughbred horses running behind a sticked-up carrot.

Noble knew how bad he had hurt Zsa Zsa, but he didn't know how to make it better. He'd peeped her walking around writing tickets on the streets, and he could tell she wasn't happy. Her body moved differently. That spark that used to glow in her eyes looked dim. It was like the light had gone out in both of their lives.

It was starting to get cold outside and Noble knew how much she hated her job in the winter. He'd sent a text message telling her he wanted to help her start her own business, and she'd sent one back that said *fuck you.* He'd had roses and balloons delivered to her house every day for a week, and she had refused the delivery each time.

He'd run across Sissy and Malisha too. Sissy, when he went to his aunt's crib and had her locks changed and switched her bills into his name to be paid from his account, and Malisha when he swung by Omega Bank and closed out all his accounts, to include his safety deposit box.

And Kiki?

Noble almost laughed. He'd seen her ass too.

All of it.

Kiki had gotten fired from her job and was stripping for a living now. Pap had dragged Noble to a titty bar in Harlem, and there Kiki was. Headlining that shit. Butt naked and swirling her hips for any man's chips.

It was funny how hard it was to peep who people really were when you were looking too hard. Noble had been forced to hold a mirror up at his own ass too, and there were a few shitty things there that he had to admit needed some work.

Months had passed since his birthday, and Noble had almost given up hope for his happiness when he opened his front door to go to work one morning and saw somebody sitting on the hood of his whip.

"Thirsty?" she asked, holding out a carton of Tropicana. It was cold as hell outside, but her smile was bright, her eyes danced, and her shiny black hair flowed down her back. The juice looked damn good too. And even from where Noble stood he could tell it was the kind that had lots of pulp.

He didn't wanna be away from her a second longer. He jammed both his crutches up under one arm, then hopped down two steps at a time tryna get to her.

"It was *you,*" Noble moaned, pulling Zsa Zsa into his arms. He nuzzled his nose deep into her warm, delicious neck. *It was always you. . . .* Leaning against the car, he inhaled everything about her that he loved and had missed so much. Wasn't no more shame in his game. He thought about that ten-carat chuck of engagement ice he'd bought and had sized just for her, and decided it was now or never.

He took the carton of orange juice from her and set it up on the Corvette's icy hood, and then answered her question.

"I'm real thirsty," Noble said, getting down on his good knee so he could propose to his number-one honey.

"Will you marry me, Zsa baby? Please say yes, because I'm thirsty for you."

Available now wherever books are sold!

Street Divas
by De'nesha Diamond

In this explosive series, the fiercest ride-or-die chicks in
Memphis are battling alongside—and against—their ruthless
men, to be the last diva standing . . .

Still a Mistress
by Tiphani Montgomery

Nothing turns Chloe on more than the luxurious perks her
slamming body earns her. And when her latest lover—a
powerful politician with sins of his own—tempts her with a
dangerous but high-paying proposition, Chloe sees more
than diamonds and cash in her future. She sees
sweet revenge . . .

Turn the page for an excerpt from these
thrilling novels . . .

1

Melanie

I'm seriously fucked. That shit hits home the second I see Python, my baby's daddy and the leader of the Black Gangster Disciples, kick down my door to see his arch enemy, Fat Ace, head nigga of the Vice Lords, giving me a good dicking down.

I'm stunned and can't move.

"WHAT THE FUCK?" Fat Ace jerks out of my pussy and makes a dive toward the nightstand for his piece.

"YOU'RE A DEAD MUTHAFUCKA!" *POW!* Python's gun sounds like a cannon.

I blink out of my trance to dive in the opposite direction just as Fat Ace starts returning fire. Right now, I'm wishing that I didn't keep my own weapon locked in a safety box at the top of my bedroom closet. Judging by the look on Python's face, Fat Ace and I aren't walking out of this muthafucka alive.

POW! POW! POW!

Python ducks and twists away from the door before Fat Ace's bullets tear huge chunks out of the door frame. Unfortunately, that leaves me in Python's direct line of vision. Time crawls the second our gazes connect, while death skips down my spine and wraps itself around my heart.

"No, Python. Wait," I beg. I even foolishly lift my hands like a stop sign as if that's really going to enforce a time-out. Python's black, empty, soulless eyes narrow. At this fucking moment, I'm no different from any other nigga on the street: disposable. I'm already dead to him, and my tears are nothing but water.

Fat Ace squeezes off another round.

POW! POW! POW!

Wood splinters from the door frame inches above Python's head, but that doesn't stop him from lifting his Glock and aiming that muthafucka straight at me. I'm a cop and I'm used to plunging headlong into danger, but I don't have a badge pinned to my titties right now, and my courage is pissing out in between my legs.

POW! POW!

Fat Ace misses again.

"Please. I'm carrying your baby." As a desperate act, I clutch the small mound below my belly, and I succeed in getting his eyes to drop.

To my left, Fat Ace's head whips in my direction. His voice booms like a clap of thunder.

"WHAT THE FUCK?"

I spin my head back toward Fat Ace. Why does it suddenly look like this muthafucka can pass for Python's twin? Anger rises off of him like steam. I open my mouth but my brain shuts down. It doesn't matter. There are no words that can save me.

"You fucking lying bitch!" Fat Ace's gun swings away from Python and toward me, while Python's gat turns toward Fat Ace. Both pull the trigger at the same time.

POW! POW!

POW! POW!

The bullets feel like two heat-seeking missiles slamming into me. I propel backward, and my head hits the wall first.

Across the room, Python's bullets slam into Fat Ace's right side, but the nigga remains on his feet and squeezes out a few more rounds.

Shocked, it takes a full second before the pain in my chest and left side has a chance to register. When it does, it's like nothing I've ever felt before. Blood gushes out of my body as I slowly slide down the wall and plop onto the floor.

POW! POW!

Python shoots the gun out of Fat Ace's hand.

POW! POW! POW!

"What, nigga? What?" Python roars.

Fat Ace clutches his bleeding hand but then charges toward Python real low and manages to tackle him to the ground before Python is able to squeeze off another shot. They hit the hardwood with a loud *thump,* and Python's gun is knocked out of his hand.

I need to get help. There's way too much blood pooling around me. *I'm dying. Me and my baby.*

"Is that all you got, nigga?" Fat Ace jams a fist into the center of Python's face. Blood bursts from Python's thick lips and big nose like a red geyser.

Tears rush down my face like a fucking waterfall. *I'm sorry, baby. I'm so sorry.* It's all I can tell my unborn child.

"Your ass gonna die tonight, you punk-ass bitch," Python growls, slamming his fist into Fat Ace's jaw.

Christopher!

My head snaps up. My son, Christopher, is in the other room. How can he sleep through all this noise? An image of Christopher, curled up in the bottom of his closet, trembling and crying, springs to my mind. *I have to get to my baby.*

I slump over from the wall but lack the strength to stop my upper body's falling momentum. My face crashes into the hard floor, and I can feel a tooth floating in blood in my mouth.

Covered in sweat and blood, Python and Fat Ace continue wrestling on the floor. Fat Ace, still naked, gets the upper hand for a second and sends a crushing blow across Python's jaw. A distinguishable *crack* reverberates in the room. To my ears, the muthafaucka should be broken, but Python ain't no ordinary nigga. And sure enough, in the next second, Python retaliates, landing one vicious blow after another. A tight swing lands below Fat Ace's rib cage. Its force not only causes another *crack,* but it also lifts Fat Ace up at least a half foot in the air and gives Python the edge in repositioning himself.

The punches flow harder and faster. The floor trembles as if we're in the middle of an earthquake. Python is shoved against the side of the bed, and the damn thing flies toward my head. Lacking the energy to get out of the way, all I can do is close my eyes and prepare for the impact. The bed's metal leg slams into the center of my forehead with a sickening *thud,* and a million stars explode behind my eyes.

The scuffling on the other side of the bed continues; more bone crushes bone. When I finally manage to open my eyes,

Python is trying to stretch his hand far enough to reach for a gun, but it is a few inches too far. Fat Ace is doing all he can to make sure that shit doesn't happen.

Watching all this go down, I realize that I don't give a fuck if they kill each other. Why should I? I'm already sentenced to death. I can feel its cold fingers settling into my bones.

More tears flow as I have my last pity party. It's true what they say—your life does flash before your eyes. But it's not the good parts. It's all the fucked-up shit that you've done. Now that judgment is seconds away, I don't have a clue what I'm going to tell the man upstairs, that's a good sign that my ass is going straight to hell.

I have to say good-bye to Christopher.

Sucking in a breath, I dig deep for some reserved strength. Determined, I drag my body across the floor, crawling with my forearms.

POW!

To my right, the bedroom window explodes, and shards of glass stab parts of my body.

Python and Fat Ace wrestle for control of the gun.

"Fuck you, muthafucka," one of them growls.

Still, I'm not concerned about their dumb asses. I need to see my baby one more time. However, I only get about half a foot before sweat breaks out across my brow and then rolls down the side of my face. How in the hell can I be cold and sweating at the same time?

POW! POW! POW!

More glass shatters. I turn my head in time to see Fat Ace's large, muscled ass dive out the window. Python runs up to the muthafucka and proceeds to empty his magazine out the broken window.

"CRABBY MUTHAFUCKA!" Python reaches into his back pocket and produces another clip. He peers out into the darkness for a minute. "I'ma get his punk ass," he says, and then turns and races out of the bedroom in hot pursuit, nearly kicking me in the head as he passes.

Relieved that he's gone, I drag myself another inch before my arms wobble and threaten to collapse. I need to catch my breath.

POW! POW! POW!

The shooting continues outside. In the distance, I hear police sirens. Then again, it could be wishful thinking. It's not like the department would respond this fuckin' fast.

Christopher. I gotta get to my baby.

Convinced that I've caught my second wind, I attempt to drag myself again. I try and try, but I can't move another inch. A sob lodges in my throat as I hear the sound of footsteps. *Christopher!* He must've gotten the courage to come see if I'm all right. "Baby, is that you?" Damn. That one question leaves me breathless. I'm panting so hard I sound like I just ran a marathon.

The slow, steady footsteps draw closer.

"Baby?" I stretch out a blood-covered hand. When I see it, I'm suddenly worried about what Christopher will think seeing me like this. Shakily, I look around. I'm practically swimming in my own piss and blood. It could scare the shit out of him, scar him for life.

He's almost at the door.

Tell him not to come in here!

"Baby, um—"

"Your fuckin' baby is gone."

Python's rumbling baritone fills my bedroom and freezes what blood I have left in my veins. My head creeps back around, and I'm stuck looking at the bottom of a pair of black jeans and shit kickers. More tears rush to my eyes. This nigga is probably going to stomp my ass into the hardwood floors.

"You're one slick, muthafuckin' bitch, you know that?"

"Python—"

"How long you been fuckin' that crab, huh?"

My brain scrambles, but I can't think of a goddamn thing to say.

"What? Cat got your tongue?" The more he talks, the deeper his voice gets. The sob that's been stuck in the middle of my throat now feels like a fucking boulder, blocking off my windpipe.

Python squats down. I avoid making eye contact because I'm more concerned about the Glock dangling in his hand. My heart should be hammering, but instead I don't think the muthafucka is working.

The gun moves toward me until the barrel is shoved underneath my chin, forcing my head up. Now it doesn't seem possible that I've spent so many years loving this nigga. How does a woman fall in love with death?

Python is not easy on the eyes, and his snake-forked tongue doesn't help. Big and bulky, his body is covered with tats of pythons, teardrops, names of fallen street soldiers, but more important is the big six-pointed star that represents the Black Gangster Disciples. He's not just a member. In this shitty town, he's the head nigga in charge—and my dumb ass crossed him.

"Look at me," he commands.

My gaze crashes into his inky black eyes, where I stare into a bottomless pit.

"You know you fucked up, right?"

I whimper and try to plea with my eyes. It's all I can do.

Muscles twitch along Python's jawline as he shakes his head. Then I see some shit that I ain't never seen before from this nigga: tears. They gloss his eyes, but they don't roll down his face. He ain't that kind of nigga.

"You fuckin' betrayed me. Out of all the niggas you could've fucked you pick that greasy muthafucka?"

"P-P-P—"

"Shut the fuck up! I don't wanna hear your ass beggin' for shit. Your life is a wrap. Believe that!" He stares into my eyes and shakes his head. "What? You thought your pussy was so damn good that I was going to let this shit slide? I got street-walkers who can pop pussy better than you. You ain't got a pot of gold buried up in that ass. I kept your triflin' ass around because I thought . . ." He shakes his head again and the tears dry up or had I imagined those muthafuckas?

Sirens. I'm sure this time. The police are coming.

He chuckles. "What? You think the brothahs and sistahs in blue are about to save your monkey ass? Sheeiiit. That ain't how this is going down."

So many tears are rolling out my eyes I can barely see him now. I want to beg again, but I know it's useless. Time to buck up. Face this shit head-on.

"I can't believe that I *ever* thought you were my rib. You ain't good enough to wipe the shit out the crack of my ass," he sneers, releasing my chin and standing up.

The next thing I hear is the unzipping of his black jeans. "You wanna live, bitch? Hmm?"

I nod but he still grabs a fistful of my hair and yanks me up. Next thing I know, his fat cock is slapping me in the face.

"Suck that shit. Show me how much you wanna fuckin' live, bitch. You fuck this shit up, and I'll blast your goddamn brains all over this fuckin' floor. You got that?"

I try to nod again, but the shit is impossible. Python's dick is so hard when he shoves that muthafucka into my mouth that he takes out another fuckin' tooth. I can't even say that I'm sucking his shit as much as I'm bleeding and choking on it.

"Sssssss." He grinds his hips and then keeps hammering away. "C'mon, pig. Get this nut."

I don't know how in the hell I remain conscious, but I do, hoping this nigga will come sooner rather than later. But when Python's dick springs out of my mouth, I'm not blasted with a warm load of salty cum but with a hot stream of nasty-ass piss. I close my mouth and try to turn my head away, but this nigga holds me still and tries to drown my ass.

"Open up, bitch. OPEN THE FUCK UP!"

Crying, I open my mouth.

"Yeah. That's right. Drink this shit up. This is the kind of nut you deserve!"

By the time he lets my head go, I'm drenched from head to goddamn toe but still sobbing and trying to cling to life.

Python stuffs his still-rock-hard dick back into his pants and zips up. "Fuckin' pathetic. That had to be the worst head I ever had."

My eyes drop to the space in between his legs. There I see my seven-year-old baby, Christopher. He stands in his pajamas, clutching his beloved teddy bear. "I'm so sorry," I whisper.

Christopher's eyes round with absolute horror.

He's going to watch me die.

"You're a fuckin' waste of space, bitch. Go suck the devil's dick," Python hisses, and then plants his gun at the back of my head and pulls the trigger.

From *Still A Mistress*

1

Chloe

"I want that bitch dead!" was the first thing he said about his mistress after cumming on top of my stomach. The murder that rested in his eyes revealed how serious he actually was as he collapsed on the bed. His sour, stale breath seemed to have climbed on my face as his breathing got heavier. He continued to lie next to me, while I looked over his shoulders and saw the culprit, a large bottle of expensive whiskey. Macallan 17 to be exact.

The bottle, which was only sips away from being empty, sat on the table. It told me that he was pissy drunk, but he held his liquor well. Most crooked politicians did.

Asheville, North Carolina's most hated mayor had made a request of me that wasn't in my job description. But as he kept talking, I found myself up for the task, and besides, the longer he talked, the more expensive the perks got. I'd been offered any luxury vehicle of my choice, a house that was big enough for a small army, and an all-day shopping spree at Bergdorf Goodman.

My nipples became even stiffer every time he mentioned an elaborate perk. I was that much closer to closing the deal, and the thought of being a murderess for hire was intriguing to me. I figured that it wouldn't hurt to add another skill to my résumé, other than fucking everybody. Besides, I could use the practice. This contract was definitely what I needed to prepare me for my next big plan.

"Chloe," he said, looking at me with glassy eyes. "I really like you, and once she's out of the way, I want you to step up."

I let out a slight laugh. "Step up? Who the fuck do you think you're talking to?" I asked. "I don't step up. I move bitches aside!"

"No, baby, I didn't mean it like that," he blurted out in an attempt not to piss me off. "It's just that you do things for me that nobody has ever done, and I want to make sure that you stay by my side."

Bullshit.

Everything that he'd just said was 100 percent bullshit. I wanted to ask him what made tonight different. What sparked the sudden change of heart? Why did he want to finally make me his main bitch? We'd been fucking for a little over six months now, and he'd never said this to me before, even though I knew he was pussy whipped.

My shit was powerful.

I was sure it was the liquor talking, and I wasn't upset at his suggestion for my new role, because the only position I'd ever played was the one of a mistress. Hell, I enjoyed being a mistress. It was the only thing I knew how to do. The thought of fucking men who belonged to other women was the ultimate turn-on. Especially since there were no strings attached, and I always got the same benefits or even more. I wouldn't even know how to be a housewife.

It was just the fact that he thought he was doing me some type of fucking favor that made me mad. Maybe he felt that pacifying me would make murdering his former mistress easier. Little did he know that he could've saved his breath. His weak promises of love didn't matter, because money was my motivator.

"By your side, huh?" I looked at him and rolled my eyes at the thought of what his plan was once he was through with me. His sorry ass would probably do me the same way. "Baby, I would never leave you," I mustered up, giving him a brief kiss on his cheek. If this was the game he wanted to play, I was down.

"That's what I want to hear," he responded.

"What about your wife? Where does she stand?" I asked even though I didn't give a fuck.

"My wife stays for now," he said, with remorse in his tone. I poked out my lower lip, pretending to be upset with his decision. "Don't worry, though. I'll never treat you like my mistress. I'll always treat you like number one."

That was all I needed to hear. "So, why do you want this woman out of your life?"

I tried my best not to get personal, but my nosiness took over, and I had questions that needed to be answered. The mayor's breath was on fire, and the scent almost melted my nose off as he continued.

"This bitch has been trying to ruin my life from the beginning, and now with her getting pregnant on purpose, I know things are about to get ugly. I want her ass dead before my wife and the public find out. She's already promised to black-mail me, and I need her stopped before it's too late!"

I inserted my index finger into my wet pussy, pulled it out, and rubbed it against his full lips. "How do you know that I won't ruin your life?"

His smile could be seen a mile away. "Because I trust you, baby. Besides, there simply isn't enough room for the both of you, and she's the one I want out of the picture. I couldn't imagine you gone."

There you go again with more bullshit, I thought. This dude must think I'm some type of rookie. Game recognizes game, and I was a professional when it came down to this shit. I knew in the end, he wouldn't give a fuck about me. It would always be about his wife.

"I'm glad you chose me, Daddy," I replied in an assuring tone.

We snuggled on his beautiful white goose-down duvet at his cottage on the Biltmore estate. This was a piece of luxury that not even his rich-ass socialite wife knew about. The only part of the house that I despised was the two-story library, which held thousands of books. It was an instant memory of my bitch-ass sister, Oshyn. Ever since we were little, books had always been her first love. Long ago I waged a war against anything she loved, and literature of any kind had now become my enemy.

I'd made myself at home in Asheville a year ago, right after I left Raleigh. I needed to get out of town after all the chaos, but I also wanted to stay as close as I could to Oshyn. My plan was to get her back for everything she'd done to me. I'd never been to Asheville before, and the mountains seemed to clear my head. Shit, even Oklahoma City bomber Timothy McVeigh came here to hide, so I knew there had to be something special about the place. There wasn't any drama here, any worries, or any problems . . . or so I thought.

I was renting a cabin and was down to my last two hundred dollars when I met the mayor at a restaurant downtown. I knew it was only a matter of time before he would be taking care of me, but I had no idea he would be the one to bring back my killer instincts.

"You're so much prettier than that other bitch I deal with," he said, stroking my hair. "And your body is to die for!"

I looked at his small gray Afro and smiled. I knew he was referring to my perky 36C cups and big, round ass. "Is she white?" I asked.

He seemed surprised by my question. "Why would you ask me that? Besides, what difference does it make?"

"Actually, I couldn't care less, but I'm just curious. For some reason, you look like the type of black man who would have a white girl on the side. Shit, I'm probably the closest thing to black pussy you've ever had. You're probably tired of being with a woman with an ironing board for an ass."

"Well, if you must know, yes, she's white."

I wasn't surprised by his comment, but I hated that I had to kill someone who sounded like a woman after my own heart. I started feeling kind of bad that I had to betray one of my fellow blackmailers. Women in this business had to stick together, but I was sure she would do the same thing if she were in my shoes. It was always business before pleasure.

My thoughts were distracted by what looked like a large, deforming burn that was shaped like the boot of Italy, sitting on the right side of his face. The miniature country, which had melted away on his brown skin, was too gross to ignore. I tried my best to avoid that side of his face when we got together, but it was hard not to look at. Something about this monstrous feature scared me.

Reminded me of the boogeyman.

Reminded me of my past.

My childhood always had a way of doing that. I tried not to let it bother me too much, because he was filthy . . . filthy rich!

I'd done my research, so I knew mayors normally didn't make tons of money, but this one did. With his sleazy political connections he netted millions in various crooked investment deals, and his ties to the mob didn't hurt his rapidly growing pockets, either.

"How much?" I whispered while rubbing his huge potbelly. After recalling all of the wealth I was surrounded by, I was ready to seal this deal, but I needed him to be as comfortable as possible with his decision.

He sat up, took another swig of his whiskey, and said, "A hundred thousand."

I paused and thought about accepting the offer, but my mind quickly wandered away again and got the best of me. I couldn't believe a hundred grand was all his mistress was worth. She was also carrying his unborn child, and he wanted them both to disappear. I immediately saw myself in her.

It was only a year ago that Oshyn had stolen my baby's life, and now I had agreed to do it to someone else. A little bit of emotion started to rise in my chest, but I quickly suppressed it. Emotion wasn't part of my résumé. If this was what he wanted, the bitch would simply have to go.

Not only did I need the money, but this would also make what I planned on doing to Oshyn a total walk in the park. I was sure that no one knew whether I was dead or alive, even after everyone died at Oshyn's house, except me and her. I'd left her home that night bullet ridden and broke. All the money I'd stacked up went right down the drain, and Brooklyn was the reason for most of it. I'd given Brooklyn the million dollars I'd blackmailed from Mr. Bourdeaux, and he took it all, leaving me with nothing.

Since then, my more generous clients had offered me permanent housing in their mansions and penthouses, but I reluctantly declined their offers. From the bullet hole Oshyn had put in my stomach to the one Brooklyn had put in my shoulder, along with the broken nose I sported, all those things were just too much to explain. With all these gunshot wounds, I was starting to feel like a female version of 50 Cent. As it turned out, I definitely had more than nine lives, minus the budding music career.

"Is a hundred thousand enough?" the mayor asked, probably uncomfortable with my long pause.

"Nah, you're gonna have to come larger than that. I'll do the bitch for a hundred, but the baby is gonna cost you another two, making it three hundred even."

"Two hundred thousand for a fucking kid that's not even born? You're out of your damn mind, Chloe. Abortions don't even cost a tenth of that!" He became enraged, and the alcohol didn't help.

"Three hundred. Take it or leave it, but it's my final offer." Even though I could've really used the hundred grand, my offer was set in stone, and I wouldn't take anything less. I just couldn't bring myself to kill the baby for anything less, born or not. Maybe with me being twenty-six now, I was beginning to gain a conscience, but this was something that truly bothered me. "Take it or leave it," I said again.

"All right. Three hundred, but not a dime more than that. After everything is done, I need you to skip town for a few weeks. You know, just until everything cools down. I've already arranged for your trip to Jamaica."

"Jamaica? That wasn't in my plans. I have things to do," I whined.

"Baby, just trust me," he begged with a sinister smile that screamed just the opposite.

That was the problem. . . . I didn't trust anybody.